HARL...
Pre...

Take a look at our b...

A marriage ended or a marriage mended? Kayla
has been bought back by her estranged husband,
billionaire Duardo Alvarez, in Helen Bianchin's
scorcher *Purchased by the Billionaire*. Bedded
for revenge or wedded for passion? Freya has
made the mistake of hiding the existence of Italian
Enrico Ranieri's little son, and she must make amends
as his convenient wife in Michelle Reid's torrid tale
The Ranieri Bride. Is revenge sweet? Greek tycoon
Christos Carides certainly thinks so when he seduces
Becca Summer in Kim Lawrence's sizzling story,
The Carides Pregnancy. But for how long? Out for
the count? Italian aristocrat Alessio Ramontella
certainly thinks he's KO'd innocent English beauty
Laura, but will she actually succumb to his ruthless
seduction? Find out in *The Count's Blackmail Bargain*
by Sara Craven. Meantime, Carol Marinelli's mixing
business with intense pleasure in her new UNCUT
novel, *Taken for His Pleasure*. It's a gold band of
blackmail for temporary bride Maddison as she's
forced to marry wealthy Greek Demetrius Papasakis
in *The Greek's Convenient Wife* by Melanie Milburne.
Mistress material? Nora Lang doesn't think she's got
what it takes in Susan Napier's *Mistress for a Weekend*.
But tycoon Blake MacLeod thinks Nora definitely has
something special—confidential information. And
he'll keep her in his bed to prevent her giving it away.
Finally, an ultimatum...*The Marriage Ultimatum* by
Helen Brooks. It's Carter Blake's only option when
Liberty refuses to let him take her.

*Legally wed,
but he's never said,
"I love you."
They're...*

**The series where marriages are made
in haste...and love comes later.**

*Look out for more WEDLOCKED!
wedding stories available only from
Harlequin Presents®.*

Helen Bianchin

PURCHASED BY THE BILLIONAIRE

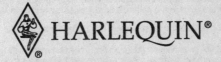

TORONTO • NEW YORK • LONDON
AMSTERDAM • PARIS • SYDNEY • HAMBURG
STOCKHOLM • ATHENS • TOKYO • MILAN • MADRID
PRAGUE • WARSAW • BUDAPEST • AUCKLAND

ISBN-13: 978-0-373-12563-0
ISBN-10:   0-373-12563-1

PURCHASED BY THE BILLIONAIRE

First North American Publication 2006.

www.eHarlequin.com

Printed in U.S.A.

All about the author...
Helen Bianchin

Helen grew up in New Zealand, an only child possessed by a vivid imagination and a love for reading. After four years of legal secretarial work, Helen embarked on a working holiday in Australia where she met her Italian-born husband, a tobacco sharefarmer in far north Queensland. His command of English was pitiful, and her command of Italian was nil. Fun? Oh yes! So too was being flung into cooking for workers immediately after marriage, stringing tobacco and living in primitive conditions.

It was a few years later when Helen, her husband and their daughter returned to New Zealand, settled in Auckland and added two sons to their family. Encouraged by friends to recount anecdotes of her years as a tobacco sharefarmer's wife living in an Italian community, Helen began setting words on paper and her first novel was published in 1975.

Creating interesting characters and telling their stories remains as passionate a challenge for Helen as it did in the beginning of her writing career.

Spending time with family, reading and watching movies are high on Helen's list of pleasures. An animal lover, Helen says her Maltese terrier and two Birman cats regard her study as much theirs as hers.

CHAPTER ONE

'You did…what?'

Kayla's features paled as consternation meshed with disbelief, then magnified into a sense of dread.

'You think it was easy for me to go to Duardo Alvarez and *beg*?' Defensive anger rose to the surface, and something else…rage.

Jacob's words fell with hammer-like pain, and for a few brief seconds she hovered between retaliatory anger and despair.

Duardo Alvarez.

The mention of his name was enough to send ice slithering down the length of her spine.

Bad boy made good, now billionaire entrepreneur with homes in several major cities around the world.

Her ex-husband…and the last person on earth likely to help her, or her brother.

'Why in hell would you do that?'

'I had no choice!' Jacob's expression revealed a torment that twisted her stomach muscles into a painful ball.

Oh, dear God.

The last time she'd seen her ex-husband had been at her father's funeral. A deeply sorrowful occasion with few genuine mourners, several curiosity-seekers…and she'd been too stunned with shocked grief to do anything other than act on autopilot.

She hadn't had contact with Duardo since. Didn't want any.

'Dammit, Jacob! How *could* you?'

He didn't answer. But then he had no need.

And right now there was no time for further argument or castigation. In nine minutes she had to catch a train into the city. Or be late.

Kayla caught up her jacket, slung the strap of her bag over one shoulder and turned towards him. 'We'll continue this discussion later.'

Jacob offered a slip of paper. 'Duardo's number. Call him by midday.'

Hell would freeze over first.

'Please.' Jacob's eyes were dark, desperate, and she pocketed the number.

'You ask too much.' Way too much. More than she could give.

Without a further word she left the small two-bedroom walk-up for the hard inner-city pavement in one of the city's less salubrious suburbs. Old terraced houses lined the street, each in various stages of decay and neglect.

A far cry from her former life.

Five years ago the Enright-Smythe family had numbered high among Sydney's rich and famous. Kayla, at twenty-two, held a degree in business management and had took out a handsome salary for a token position in the 'firm'.

A member of the 'young social-set', she attended every party in town, spent an outrageous sum on clothes, travelled, and was seen on the arm of a different man every week.

Until Duardo Alvarez entered the field.

In his mid-thirties and cloaked in sophistication, on the rise within the city's financial sector, his youthful past hinted at association with the shady underbelly of New York.

He was everything Kayla's parents didn't want for their only daughter.

All the more reason, in her year of tilting at windmills, coupled with boredom, for deliberately setting Duardo in her sights.

He excited her. So, too, did a sense of the forbidden. Winning him over became a game. Holding him off took enormous self-restraint. She succeeded, and in a moment of sheer madness she accepted his proposal to fly to Hawaii and marry him.

Seventy-two hours later the marriage was over.

Courtesy of Benjamin Enright-Smythe's ultimatum and her mother's death...a heart attack which put Blanche Enright-Smythe into Intensive Care and took her life.

A tragic loss for which Benjamin attributed the blame to his daughter, referring privately and publicly to the marriage as *Kayla's folly*.

Her father's denunciation speared a stake through Kayla's heart and left her racked with guilt at the thought that her whirlwind marriage might have contributed to Blanche's death. Confidante and friend, Blanche had always been there for her, frequently acting as a calming buffer between two clashing personalities...Benjamin's arrogance and Kayla's defiance.

In the devastating numbness that followed Blanche's funeral, she stood at her father's side, comforted Jacob and somehow managed to get through each day. Wanting, needing the comfort of the one man who could help ease her grief...her husband.

Medical results indicated Blånche had been dealing with heart disease for some time, evidence Benjamin refused to accept in his demented quest to wreak revenge on the man he blamed for Blanche's death.

It proved a heart-wrenching time, with divided loyalties whittling away at Kayla's emotional heart. She was painfully aware of Benjamin's fragile mental state and Jacob's need for comfort and stability.

How could she give her personal life priority at such a time?

Yet how long could she expect Duardo to be patient? Benjamin's ultimatum—*Leave this house, and you'll never be welcome inside it again*—almost tore her in two.

Family. Something her mother had considered to be sacrosanct.

Except Benjamin was hell-bent on denigration, dredging up written proof that acquisition of the Enright-Smythe empire was part of Duardo's agenda. And that Kayla had merely been a pawn in his game plan.

That day something within her withered and died.

She refused Duardo's calls, acceded to her father's demands that Duardo be forbidden entry to the family home.

Then Duardo issued an ultimatum of his own.

Choose. Your husband or your family.

She didn't utter so much as a word beneath Benjamin's torrent of anger. Instead, she slid off her wedding band and handed it to the man whose name she'd taken as her own. And watched him turn and walk away.

Then she witnessed, in the ensuing months, Duardo Alvarez's acquisition of the Enright-Smythe business empire, with Duardo now firmly labeled a predator with one goal in mind.

Absent was the desire to party, and Kayla's friends

gradually gave up issuing invitations as she refused each and every one of them. The association with frivolity and flirtatious fun seemed firmly embedded in pain. The kind of pain she never wanted to suffer again in her lifetime.

The only social occasions she attended were those instigated by her father: dull, boring business dinners where she was forced to watch Benjamin's decline among his peers.

Within a year, the firm of Enright-Smythe held a list of unfulfilled contracts, union problems, and was the subject of a takeover bid by none other than Duardo Alvarez.

By then everything had been auctioned off…the family home, staff, the Bentley, her mother's jewellery, works of art.

The media made much of it at the time.

Benjamin proceeded to gamble his way into bankruptcy, only to compound his fall from grace by committing suicide. This tragic act devastated Kayla and sent Jacob into a downward spiral of despair.

For the past three years she'd worked her day job, waitressing in a local restaurant five hours each night and on weekends in an effort to keep a roof over their heads and help pay off a mountain of debt.

Jacob put in similar hours, quitting university at nineteen and abandoning all hope of entering medical school.

Yet it wasn't enough. It would never be enough. And the money-lenders were closing in. No thanks to her brother, who in an act of desperation had played the casino, and lost.

Forget the banks, she had no collateral. Everything she'd owned of any worth had been sold. And her working hours were at a maximum.

The entrance to the subway loomed, and she rode the escalator, saw the train and watched with a sense of fatalism as it pulled away from the station.

A hollow laugh rose and died in her throat.

How much worse could the day get?

It was unwise to tempt Fate, even in humour. Add cynicism, and it could turn round and bite you, Kayla reflected as she dealt with irate phone calls, negotiated a peaceful solution between two aggressive staff members and soothed a client who threatened to take his business elsewhere unless his demands were met.

Yoghurt and fruit eaten at her desk sufficed as lunch, and the afternoon involved a series of meetings, both in-house and via conference calls.

It was after five when she shut down the laptop, relieved this part of the day was over.

Not the night, Kayla reflected wearily as she collected her bag and slung the strap over one shoulder.

A forty-five-minute time-frame was all she had in which to catch a train and report for work at an Italian restaurant in her local shopping centre. Working there offered the bonus of supplying her with a meal, usually eaten on the run between serving customers, and it was within walking distance of home.

The phone on her desk rang, and she hesitated over answering it. Whoever it was, she decided as she picked up the handset, she'd give them two minutes, tops, then she was out the door.

'Thank God I caught you,' a familiar male voice breathed in relief.

'Jacob?' Something was wrong. She could sense it, almost feel it.

'I won't be home tonight.' His voice was jerky. 'Hospital. Smashed kneecap.'

'Which hospital?' She stifled an inaudible groan as he cited one on the other side of the city. 'I'll be there as soon as I can.'

'Call Duardo, Kayla. I don't need to spell out *why*.'

Ice ran through her veins as he cut the connection.

A smashed kneecap as a warning? What next, broken ribs, damaged kidneys, wrecked spleen? How long would the thugs wait before they meted out another *lesson*? A few days? A week?

Her financial situation wasn't going to change. Heaven knew how long it would take for Jacob to return to work. Without his wages to complement her own, together with a swathe of medical bills…it was hopeless.

Kayla closed her eyes, then opened them again.

The slip of paper Jacob had handed her this morning was in her jacket pocket. She retrieved it, punched in the series of digits and waited for Duardo to answer.

What if he knew where she worked, and recognized the number on caller ID? Worse, what if he chose not to pick up?

'Alvarez.'

The sound of his voice curled round her nerve-ends, tugged a little and almost robbed her of the ability to speak.

'It's Kayla.' Oh, dear heaven, how could she go through with this?

His silence seemed to reverberate down the line.

'I need your help.'

Would he agree, or sever communication?

'My office.' He gave precise directions. 'Ten minutes.' And he ended the call.

She reconnected, only to have the call go to voicemail.

He was pulling her strings. It irked unbearably that he *could*. Dammit. She had the irresistible urge to throw something, preferably at *him*.

Given it was impossible for her to be in three different

places at once, she rang the restaurant, relayed the reason why she'd be late, promised to be there as soon as she could and listened to a heated response.

It was all she needed right now to be in the firing line of rapidly spoken Italian ire, soothed only in conclusion by expressed sympathy for her brother's accident.

Kayla emerged onto the pavement and cast an eye at the leaden sky. *Rain*, why don't you? Make my day!

Almost in direct response, the first raindrops fell. Great big fat ones, increasing with a speed and intensity that showed no intention of abating any time soon.

Great. So now she'd face her ex-husband looking very much like a drowned rat.

The price of an evening newspaper helped ward off the worst of the downpour, and some ten minutes later she entered the impressive marble lobby of one of the city's glass and steel architecturally designed office buildings, ditched the sodden paper and rode the lift to the top floor.

Alvarez Holdings occupied an executive suite, which at first sight appeared to cover the entire floor, Kayla perceived as she took in the thick tinted glass, luxurious fittings, furnishings and the latest technology.

A perfectly groomed young woman manned Reception. Moonlighting as a model for *Vogue*?

Stop with the cynicism.

Image, she reminded herself, was everything, and Duardo Alvarez could afford whatever image he chose to project on planet Earth.

'Kayla Smythe.' She'd left off the preceding hyphenated *Enright* some time ago. 'I have an appointment with—' she hesitated fractionally. This was business, not personal— 'Mr Alvarez.'

The answering smile held polite warmth…practised, and tuned up or down according to client importance. In this instance, down a notch.

'Mr Alvarez is unavoidably detained in conference.' She indicated the bay of comfortable chairs. 'If you'd care to take a seat?'

Kayla felt her stomach tighten with nervous tension. Now that she was here, she wanted it over and done with.

Each passing minute seemed like ten, and she had to make a conscious effort not to constantly check her watch. She idly flipped the pages of a complimentary magazine, with no recollection of absorbing script or pictures.

How long would she have to wait?

Was Duardo Alvarez stretching out the time to deliberately unnerve her?

If she could walk out of here, she thought darkly… Yet doing so would achieve nothing. And this wasn't about *her*, she reminded herself.

'Kayla.'

She glanced up at the sound of her name and saw the receptionist move out from the console.

'Mr Alvarez will see you now.'

Stand tall and project a semblance of aloof confidence. The latter was almost impossible, given the state of her nerves.

She'd seen his image on the television screen, in newspapers and photographs in glossy magazines. But it was *years* since she had come face-to-face with him.

Would he look the same?

The silent query arose in a moment of sheer hysteria, and she beat it down as she followed the receptionist along a wide passageway to a set of imposing double doors.

Calm. She had to remain calm and in control.

Who was she kidding? She was as nervous as a kitten about to walk on hot coals, and at that moment she hated him, herself…most of all she hated the situation which had brought her here.

The receptionist placed a discreet knock on one of the doors, turned the knob and pushed the door open, announced Kayla's presence with smooth efficiency, then retreated.

She stood frozen, limbless, as she focused on the dark-suited figure standing silhouetted against the wide floor-to-ceiling plate glass.

From this distance, with the late-afternoon light behind him, it was difficult to define his expression.

Then he turned towards her, and the breath caught in her throat.

Tall, with an admirable breadth of shoulder, he projected an enviable aura of power most men coveted, but few possessed.

Well-defined facial bone structure, harshly chiselled, portrayed an elemental ruthlessness that visibly warned he was a force to be reckoned with in any arena.

'Come in and shut the door.' His drawl held a hint of cynicism, his appraisal ruthlessly unequivocal as he took in her petite stature, the blonde hair swept high and damp from the rain.

What happened to *hello*? But what did she expect…polite civility?

'You must know I don't want to be here.'

'Point taken.' He indicated a button-backed leather chair. 'Sit down.'

And have him tower over her? 'I'd prefer to stand.'

His expression didn't change, yet she gained the fleeting impression something deep within him uncoiled in readiness to strike.

'I don't have much time.' Oh, hell, she didn't want to sound defensive. Yet everything about him screamed out for her to turn and run as far and as fast as she could.

He crossed the room to stand within touching distance, and this close she saw the tiny lines fanning from each corner of those dark, almost black eyes. The grooves slashing each cheek seemed to etch a little deeper than she remembered, and that mouth...

Dear heaven, don't even go there.

One dark eyebrow rose in silent query, and she found herself almost stumbling in speech. 'Jacob is in hospital.' Pride kept her chin high. 'I'm sure you have no difficulty imagining *why*?'

Each passing second seemed to stretch until the silence became a palpable entity. 'Your brother isn't going anywhere in a hurry.' He waited a beat. 'Neither are you.'

Sapphire eyes flashed with brilliant blue fire. 'I beg your pardon?'

Down, but not cowed, Duardo perceived. She didn't disappoint.

'Let's dispense with the pretense, shall we?' When it came to game-playing, he was a lifetime ahead of her. 'You have a mountain of debt you can't hope to clear in a lifetime. Thugs have served the first of a few painful lessons for late payment. And you have no one else but me to turn to.'

Her eyes hardened. 'Does it give you pleasure to know that?'

'You can choose to walk out that door now,' he intoned with deceptive quiet.

'And if I do?'

'You'll never walk through it again.'

His words held a frightening finality, leaving her in no doubt he meant every one of them.

She had a mental picture of Jacob lying in an open coffin, instead of a hospital bed, and she was unable to control the shiver of fear slithering down her spine.

'Perhaps we can start over?'

Benjamin had done a number on her. His own daughter. At the time Duardo had wanted to haul her over his shoulder and take her away. Vilify her father, and sue for defamation of character. Instead, he'd worked behind the scenes, and achieved what Benjamin had falsely accused him of at the time.

Because he could.

Now he moved to lean one hip against the edge of his desk, and watched her struggle for composure.

'Jacob told me you're aware of our…situation.'

He wasn't going to make it easy. But then, why should he?

What they'd shared…what once had been…was now long gone. Destroyed by complex circumstances.

'You want my help,' Duardo prompted with silky smoothness, and caught the glitter of helpless anger in those brilliant blue eyes. It gave him no pleasure to see it there.

'Yes.'

Would he make her beg? *Could* she?

For Jacob. Survival. Because she had no choice.

'We need money.' Oh, hell, this was hard. 'To pay some debts.'

'Debts which will soon accumulate and escalate to a repeat of this situation within a very short space of time.'

He knew. He had to know. Jacob would have told him, and it wouldn't take much to access the true state of their miserably dire state of affairs.

She wanted to weep, but strong women don't succumb to emotional distress.

'Please.' Desperation fractured her voice.

'There are conditions.'

She expected no less. 'What do you propose?' Inside she was a mess of jangling nerves.

'I clear all debts, and fund Jacob through medical school.'

Millions of dollars.

Her brother's discarded dream fulfilled.

A substantial financial package, for which payment in one form or another would have to be made.

She needed for him to spell it out. 'In return for…what?'

'I want what I once had.' He watched the realization sink in, then hammered it home. '*You*. As my wife.'

Colour leeched from her face, and for a few seconds it seemed as if the room took a slight sideways tilt.

Wife?

She had a sudden need to sit down, yet to do so would betray her vulnerability. And she refused to give him the satisfaction.

Yet there was nothing she could do about the way her heart raced to an accelerated beat at the thought of that hard, muscular body entwined with her own in intimate possession, enticing, sharing…gifting the ultimate tactile pleasure, with his mouth, his hands.

As it had been during those brief few days of their marriage, when he'd introduced her to the sensual delights of the flesh, and she'd believed herself to be *in love* and loved.

Even now she experienced dreams so exquisitely sensual she woke bathed in sweat…and *wanting*.

Kayla could only look at him, aware to a frightening degree of his strength of will and the power he wielded.

'Revenge, Duardo?'

He took his time in answering. 'Everything has a price.' Eyes as dark as sin seared her own. 'My terms,' he enforced with dangerous silkiness. 'Accept or reject them.'

Commit herself to him, accept him into her body, play at being *wife*…

'For how long?' The query fell from her lips.

'As long as it takes.'

Until he tired of her? Live on a knife-edge, waiting for the figurative axe to fall?

She couldn't do it.

Yet what choice did she have?

None. Zilch. *Nada*.

A pulse hammered at the edge of her throat as she fought the temptation to turn and walk out the door, out of his office…his life.

It didn't help that he knew. Or that he was intent on playing a deliberate game, pushing her buttons…simply because he could.

'I hate you.' Her voice was a vengeful whisper dredged up from the depths of her soul.

'For reclaiming you as my wife?'

'For using me as human collateral.'

'Careful, *querida*.' His warning held a dangerous silkiness that mocked the endearment.

She almost told him to go to hell.

Almost.

Only the vivid image of Jacob lying injured in a hospital bed, and the very real implication of what would inevitably follow without a large injection of cash stopped her wayward tongue.

There was only one way out of this mess. Only one man who could help.

'You want me to write it in blood?'

He didn't pretend to misunderstand. 'Your acceptance?'

Her eyes flashed with brilliant blue fire. 'Yes, damn you!'

Duardo pushed himself away from the edge of his desk in a single fluid movement and closed the space between them. 'Your gratitude is underwhelming.'

'What did you expect? For me to fall on my knees at your feet?'

'Now, there's an evocative thought.' His drawl held a degree of cynical humour, and brought a rush of colour to her cheeks.

Dignity. She reined it in and with her head held high she moved back a pace. 'Are you done? I need to go see Jacob, then get to work.'

She walked towards the door, pausing halfway to look back over her shoulder. 'I imagine you'll be in touch when the legalities are in place?'

He hadn't moved, yet she had the impression his hard-muscled body was coiled, ready to spring.

'There's just one thing,' Duardo declared with hateful ease. 'The deal is effective immediately.'

'Excuse me?'

He extracted his cellphone and extended it towards her. 'Call the restaurant and terminate your employment.'

His eyes hardened as she opened her mouth to protest. 'Do it, Kayla. Or I will.'

When she refused to take the cellphone, he flipped it open and made two consecutive calls which effectively left her jobless.

The fact he knew where she worked and who to call made her want to hit him. 'Bastard,' she bit out in husky condemnation, watching as he pocketed the cellphone and moved towards her.

She was totally unprepared for the slide of his fingers

through her hair as he held fast her nape and used the flat of his hand at the back of her waist to draw her in close.

Then his mouth was on hers, taking advantage of her shocked surprise to gain entry and begin wreaking havoc with her senses in a kiss that captured and staked a shameless claim.

For a few brief, heart-stopping moments she forgot who she was, or *where*... There was only the man, his sensual power, remembered desire and an instinctive need to meet it.

Recognition, in its most primal form.

Except a part of her brain, her heart, provided an intrusive force. That was *then*...not now.

Oh, dear God.

Realisation caused her to wrench free...an action that was all the more galling because he made no attempt to stop her.

Anger, unuttered rage, showed in the glittering depths of her eyes, the tinge of colour heating her cheeks and her heaving chest as she sought to regain a degree of control.

'Now you have something to curse me for.'

She opened her mouth, but no sound emerged, and she closed it again. Wanting, needing to rail against him...physically, emotionally.

To what end?

Duardo took in her expressive features, defined each fleeting emotion and resisted the temptation to take that fine temper and tame it a little.

It helped to know that he could.

Kayla just looked at him. He wasn't even breathing deeply. How could he appear so *calm*, when she was a total mess?

'Shall we leave?'

Jacob, hospital... For a few seconds she felt stricken that both had temporarily fled her mind, and she stepped quickly into the passageway, aware Duardo easily matched her footsteps to Reception, where he bade the *Vogue* model lookalike 'goodnight', and summoned the lift.

There were words she wanted to fling at him, an inner rage threatening to eclipse rational thought. So much so, her body almost shook with it as she rode the lift down to ground level.

She told herself she should feel relieved the financial nightmare would soon be at an end. Instead, all her nerve-ends frayed into shreds as reality began to impact.

Life as she'd known it for the past few years was about to change dramatically.

The electronic cubicle came to a halt and the doors slid open to reveal the basement car park.

She needed the lobby, and she pressed the appropriate button, only to have Duardo reach forward and countermand her action.

'You're coming with me.'

'The hell I am.' Kayla's eyes flashed brilliant blue fire. 'Tomorrow is soon enough for me to be shackled to you.'

'The hospital,' he intoned with chilling softness. 'After which we transfer everything from your apartment to my home.'

'Dammit! I—'

'Walk, or be carried. Choose.'

That he meant every word was evident in those harshly chiselled features, and she almost defied him...just for the sheer hell of it.

Almost.

Instead she walked at his side, slid into the passenger seat of his top-of-the-range Aston Martin, and maintained an icy silence as he drove across town.

CHAPTER TWO

Jacob was in a large ward, his leg strapped in protective padding, and receiving pain management via a drip.

He looked pale, dejected and almost fearful in the initial seconds before Kayla entered his line of vision, then his expression lightened and he smiled as he sighted the man at her side.

Duardo Alvarez. Their white knight in shining armor. Although *dark angel* was more appropriate, she acknowledged with wry cynicism.

'Hi.' Her greeting was warm with concern as she leaned in close to brush her lips to her brother's cheek, and heard his barely audible 'thank God' seconds before she lifted her head.

In the space of what appeared to be a very short time Duardo organized for Jacob to be transferred to a private suite, engaged a team of orthopaedic surgeons and scheduled surgery.

Omnipotent power, Kayla perceived, backed by unlimited money.

She knew she should be grateful...and she assured herself she was, for Jacob's sake. It didn't mean she had to like the deal or the man who'd made it.

The Orderly arrived to effect Jacob's transfer, and she bade her brother a reluctant 'goodnight'.

'I'll be here in the morning before they take you into Theatre,' Kayla promised as the Orderly wheeled Jacob down the corridor.

It was after seven when Duardo eased the Aston Martin from the hospital car park, and the evening light was beginning to fade, tinging the pale sky with streaks of pink that gradually changed to orange as he negotiated traffic.

Soon it would be dark, and she wanted nothing more than to return to her apartment, hit the shower and fall into bed.

Except that wasn't going to happen any time soon, and the bed she'd sleep in wouldn't be her own, but *his*.

The mere thought sent heat flooding her veins, and she consciously focused on the scene beyond the windscreen in an effort to divert attention from what the night would bring.

Streetlights sprang on, vying with brightly coloured neon signs, and traffic banked up as main arterial roads linked to traverse the Harbour Bridge.

A short while later Duardo brought the car to a halt and switched off the engine.

Nothing looked familiar—not the locale, the street. 'Why did you stop here?'

'Dinner.' He freed his seat belt and climbed out from behind the wheel. 'We both need to eat.'

'I'm not hungry.'

He crossed round to her side and opened the door. 'Get out, Kayla.' When she made no effort to move he leant forward to release her seat belt.

The simple action had the breath lodging in her throat as his arm brushed her breast. He was close, much too close, and she froze, unwilling to so much as *breathe* for the few seconds it took him to complete the simple task.

Arguing with him would get her nowhere. And there was such a thing as sheer cussedness. It had been a while since lunch, and no way could the yoghurt and fruit she'd snacked on be termed a *meal*.

With that thought in mind she slid to her feet and crossed the street at his side, entering a small restaurant where the maître d' greeted Duardo by name and personally ushered them to a secluded table.

Kayla refused wine, chose soup as a starter, an entrée as a main, followed by fresh fruit.

'Would you prefer silence, or meaningless conversation?'

Duardo spared her a faintly mocking smile. 'You could begin by filling me in on the last few years.'

'Why, when you already know everything?' She lifted her water glass and took a sip of the iced liquid. 'Did you employ someone to watch my every move?'

Duardo leaned back in his chair and regarded her steadily. 'Last time I heard, it wasn't a crime for a man to retain interest in an ex-wife.'

The waiter served their soup, offered crusty bread then retreated as Kayla raked Duardo's compelling features with something akin to scorn.

'A wife you deliberately sought with an eye to the main chance.'

His expression hardened, and there was an almost frightening element evident in the depths of those dark eyes.

'Perhaps you'd care to explain that comment?'

'The Enright-Smythe consortium.'

'Indeed?'

His voice was like ice slithering in a slow slide down the length of her spine.

'Benjamin showed me written proof.'

'Impossible, given there was none at the time.'

'You're lying. I saw the letters.'

'Which you read?'

The scene flashed vividly to mind, ingrained in her mind as the moment love had died. Papers, Duardo's name. Her father's voice, loud and accusing in denunciation.

She'd skimmed the text, sightlessly, before Benjamin had flung the papers onto his study floor and stamped a foot on them.

'You can't deny you succeeded in a takeover bid for Benjamin's company.' She was like a runaway train, unable to stop. 'Did it give you pleasure to watch him sink into bankruptcy?'

His gaze didn't waiver. 'Your father's financial decline provided me with an opportunity to add to my investment portfolio. I'm a businessman. If it hadn't been me, it would have been someone else.'

'Of course,' she acknowledged with facetious intent, only to lapse into strained silence as the waiter appeared at the table to remove their soup bowls; soup she hardly remembered tasting.

'A deal brokered after the dissolution of our marriage.'

The tension escalated into a tangible entity. 'I don't believe you.'

'Any more than you can accept your father might have fabricated a tissue of lies and manufactured supposed *proof*?'

Shocked anger widened her eyes. 'He wouldn't have done that.' Her voice rose a fraction. 'I was his daughter!'

Their main meal was delivered, and served with a polite flourish.

'Benjamin's most prized possession.' Duardo waited a beat. 'One he would have done anything to remove from my orbit.'

Kayla looked at the artistically displayed food on her plate, and felt suddenly ill. 'You're wrong.'

'I, too, can produce documented proof.' He picked up a fork, speared a morsel and held it suspended for a few seconds. 'The comparison with Benjamin's papers should prove—' he paused almost perceptibly '—interesting, don't you think?'

Except there were no papers. At least, not those. When she'd asked, Benjamin had insisted they were with his lawyers. Who, on enquiry, could find no record of them.

It seemed unconscionable that Benjamin would contrive to destroy her marriage. Had his personal grief over Blanche's loss tipped him over the edge?

'Eat,' Durado commanded quietly.

'I'm not hungry.' For even a mouthful would choke her, and she pushed her plate to one side, her appetite gone.

It had been a doozy of a day. One that was far from over. She wanted to walk out of here, away from this inimical man, what he proposed…everything.

'Don't even consider it.' His tone was a silky threat, and, without thinking, she picked up her glass and flung the contents in his face.

In seeming slow motion she watched Duardo collect his table napkin, glimpsed the startled attention of the waiter, who rushed to his aid, and she stood to her feet, collected her purse…and fled.

She made the pavement, lifted a hand to flag a passing cab, only to cry out as strong hands closed over her shoulders and swung her around.

Duardo's features looked hard in the dim reflected streetlight, the structural bones etched in controlled anger.

'You're hurting me.'

'Believe me, I'm being extremely careful not to.'

For a moment the tension between them was electric, stretched so taut the slightest movement would result in an explosive shower of sparks.

'I can't do this.' It was an agonized cry dredged from the depths of her soul.

His hands slid up to cup her face, tilting it so she had no recourse but to look at him.

'I need time,' she said.

'Time won't change a thing.'

'Please.'

He traced the outline of her mouth with the edge of his thumb. 'No.'

Kayla bit him…*hard*. Heard his muffled oath, tasted his blood and cried out as he hefted her over one shoulder.

'Put me down!'

'Soon.'

She curled her hands into fists and pummelled them against his back. To no avail, as he strode easily to his car, unlocked the passenger door and bundled her into the seat.

He was close, far too close as he caught the seat belt and clipped it in place. 'Move, and I won't answer for the consequences.'

She hated him…didn't she? Hated him for placing her in this invidious position.

Yet…what if he was telling the truth?

Had her father lied and connived to his own ends?

She shook her head in disbelief. It was almost too much for her to take in.

She watched as Duardo walked around the car and slid in behind the wheel.

It was difficult to see his expression in the dim interior of the car, and she stared blankly at the night scene beyond the windscreen.

'I want to see the paperwork detailing your takeover.'

She had to *know*.

'I'll instruct my lawyer to supply you with a copy.'

The Aston Martin purred to life, and she sat in strained silence as the car traversed the city streets. Duardo offered the opportunity for a life free from debt, the fulfillment of her brother's dream.

Jacob was all she had, and he *deserved* this chance.

So, too, did she. She closed her eyes, then opened them again. For the love of God...*didn't she*?

The alternative...

Don't go there. It serves no purpose.

There was only *now*. And she'd deal with it. She *had* to.

The car drew to a halt in the narrow inner-city suburban street where she lived.

A late-model four-wheel-drive was parked nearby, and she stood still as Duardo paused to speak with the driver before indicating the entrance to her apartment.

Dim lighting didn't disguise the dingy surroundings, or the well-trodden wooden stairs as she ascended them ahead of him. Chipped paint, and the faint but distinct smell of decay.

Double locks on the door protected a pitiful space with minimal furniture, worn furnishings and the lack of personal touches. It was simply a place to sleep, not to live.

'Collect what you need.'

It didn't take long to transfer her meagre belongings into one bag and place Jacob's possessions into another. 'The landlord—'

'Spence has already dealt with it.' He indicated the small foldaway table. 'Leave the key.'

Kayla looked at him in silent askance as he caught hold of both bags.

'I made a few calls from the hospital.'

To people who were paid to jump instantly to attention at his slightest command.

Wealth…extreme wealth, she mentally corrected, had its distinct advantages.

It took only minutes to descend the stairs and pass through the shabby entrance onto the pavement. Almost instantly, a dark figure moved forward to take both bags from Duardo's grasp and deposit them in the rear of the four-wheel-drive.

'Spence.' Duardo clarified and completed the introduction before turning towards her. 'Let's go.'

Was it too late to change her mind? *Could* she?

Yes…and no.

She was barely aware of Spence sliding behind the wheel until she heard the engine engage and saw the four-wheel-drive ease away from the kerb.

There went all her worldly possessions.

Kayla spared Duardo a vengeful look that lost most of its effect in the dim evening light. 'Mind-reading is one of your talents?'

'You want to argue?' His voice was deceptively mild, yet she sensed steel beneath the surface.

'Not particularly.'

He crossed to the car, disarmed the alarm, opened the passenger door and stood waiting for her to get in.

Which she did, with considerable grace and no apparent reluctance. A lesson in the game of pretense, she accorded, aware it was the first of many she'd be required to play in the coming months.

Oh, tell it like it is, she chided silently as the car whispered through the busy streets.

Duardo had specified…*wife*.

A warm and willing body in his bed. A social hostess.

What if she fell pregnant?

A groan rose and died in her throat. Protection...she had none. Hadn't used or needed it.

'Nothing to say?'

Kayla spared his profile a steady glance. 'I'm plotting your downfall.'

His soft chuckle curled round her nerve-ends.

'You don't believe me?'

'I believe you'll try.'

'Count on it.' She glanced idly at the changing scene as the Aston Martin entered the eastern suburbs, where the inner-city shabby abodes were replaced with classy apartment buildings, well-kept homes guarded by walls and ornate gates.

Duardo, according to the media, resided in a luxurious Point Piper mansion overlooking the inner harbour, bought at the time of his marriage, but never lived in by *her*.

It was purported he'd brought in a team of builders, gutted the interior and virtually redesigned the internal structure before spending a veritable fortune on fittings and furnishings.

A fortress, Kayla observed, guarded by hi-tech security, and accessible only to those authorised to enter.

Well-positioned lighting revealed beautifully tended lawns and gardens, a curving driveway leading to an elegant mansion, and it was impossible not to feel the acceleration of nervous tension as Duardo brought the car to a halt beneath the wide portico.

One of two large double doors opened to frame a slender middle-aged woman.

'Maria,' Duardo indicated quietly as he released his seat belt. 'My housekeeper.'

Spence, Maria—

'Her husband, Josef, takes care of the grounds and maintenance.'

And Josef comprised the complement of staff. Live-in?

'There are two self-contained flats above the garages. Maria and Josef occupy one, Spence the other.'

Kayla slid out from the car, and, introductions complete, she entered the magnificent marble-tiled lobby.

Huge, with a curved double staircase leading to the upper floor, exquisite lighting, gleaming dark furniture and a number of beautifully carved wooden doors guarding various rooms.

There would, she determined, be panoramic views over the harbour during the day, with a fairyland of lights at night.

'There is coffee, or tea if you'd prefer,' the housekeeper relayed quietly and incurred Duardo's thanks. 'The bags have been taken up to the master suite.'

Kayla's stomach took a backwards flip…at least, that was what it felt like! She didn't want to *think* about the bedroom, much less go there.

'Tea would be lovely.' And a delaying tactic. 'Perhaps I could freshen up, first?'

Duardo indicated the staircase. 'Of course.'

Two different wings, one comprised of a few guest suites and an informal lounge, while the other held three bedrooms each with adjoining *en suites*, with the master suite in prominent position overlooking the harbour.

A large room, with a spacious alcove containing two comfortable chairs, an antique desk and a television cabinet. Two *en suite* bathrooms, two walk-in wardrobes.

She avoided looking at the bed…the very large bed.

'You have a beautiful home.'

'A compliment, Kayla?'

'You doubt I can gift you one?'

He shrugged out of his suit jacket and spread it over a valet frame, then he tugged off his tie and loosened the top button of his shirt before moving to the door. 'When you're ready, take the second door on your left at the base of the stairs.'

There was a sense of relief in being free from his presence. But not for long…

It would be bliss, absolute bliss to take a leisurely shower and shampoo her hair with the high-end market products lined up in the *en suite*. To use the hair-drier, wrap her body in the luxurious towelling robe, then slip into that comfortable bed…and sleep.

The temptation was too great, and with quick, economical movements she discarded her clothes, then stepped into the large marbled-tiled shower stall to luxuriate in an endless supply of steaming hot water.

The delicately scented body-wash was heaven, so, too, the luxury shampoo…neither of which she'd been able to afford to use for years.

Had Maria been instructed to stock up the *en suite*? Or were the products a complimentary gesture to whichever female Duardo took to his bed?

A man of his calibre had women falling all over him. Attracted to his wealth, his social status…and tantalized by his former bad-boy reputation.

Kayla tilted her head and let the water's needle-spray course over her face. Dammit, it felt so *good* not to have to consider a tiny heating system that permitted three-minute ablutions before the water ran cold.

It was a while before Kayla turned off the dial, then, towelled dry, she pulled on the robe before tending to her hair.

Bed had never looked so good, and she turned back the top cover, touched the feather pillow with something akin to reverence…

She should unpack—but who was she kidding? The contents of her bag were so basic it would take only minutes to stow them.

As to pulling on clothes…the idea had little appeal. Nor did returning downstairs.

The weight of the day and its outcome descended on her slim shoulders, and she slid between the fine percale sheets with care.

She wasn't going anywhere.

Duardo could come find her when *he* was ready.

Kayla slept, unaware of Duardo's presence, more than an hour later, or that he stood looking down at her pale features in repose.

She didn't register that he left the room and returned close to midnight, nor did she hear the shower or sense him slide into bed.

It was only when her hand came into contact with a solid, warm ribcage in the early hours of the morning that she freaked out, subconsciously unaware of where she was in those initial few seconds.

She knew only that it was dark, the bed wasn't her own…and *who* in hell was controlling her frantic need to escape.

She heard her name…then movement, and the room became bathed in soft light.

Son-of-a-bitch. Duardo bit back the muffled curse as he took in the tumbled hair, the heated cheeks, her heaving body, the stark fear in those brilliant blue eyes…and witnessed the moment comprehension hit.

'You forgot where you were.'

Oh, dear lord. 'Yes.' The simplicity of it seemed ludicrous.

He was close, much too close. The warmth of his skin covering hard muscle and sinew, the clean masculine scent of soap...the sensual heat that was his alone.

Physical awareness as strong as it had ever been. Riveting, hypnotic...*pagan*.

The need to put some space between them was imperative, and she moved a little, aware of the stillness apparent in the dark depths of his eyes.

He could easily reach for her, draw her in against him and cover her mouth with his own. Soothe, seduce...and have her go up in flames.

As he had, many times, during their magical time in Hawaii. An apt and willing pupil, she'd exulted beneath his skilled hands, his mouth, the feel of him deep inside her.

How many nights had she lain awake, cursing herself for allowing him to walk away? For not having the courage, the perspicacity to stand up against her father.

Now she was back in Duardo's bed for all the wrong reasons, and she hated him for it.

'Go to sleep.'

As if!

'Unless you need some help?' His drawled query was unmistakable, and she made no attempt to disguise the slight bitterness in her voice.

'Do I have a choice?'

'For now.'

'Thank heaven for small mercies.'

'Cynicism doesn't suit you.'

'Pity.' She paused as she speared his gaze with her own. 'I'm not big on warm fuzzies at the moment.'

His soft chuckle was almost her undoing. 'I seem to recall you being quite talkative at this hour of the morning.'

In the afterglow of exceptionally great sex. When she lay curled into him, her cheek nestled against his chest. A time of dreams, love, hope.

'I'm surprised you remember.' Kayla's response was deliberately tart. 'With all the women who followed me.'

'You imagine there were so many?'

Thinking about just how many was like being stabbed in the heart. 'They would have stood in line for the privilege.'

'A back-handed compliment, Kayla?'

'A statement of fact.'

'Derived from experience?'

'A trick question, Duardo?' She was damned if she'd reveal she'd taken no one to her bed…since, or before him.

A silent laugh bubbled up in her throat, almost choking her. The original virgin…a one-man woman. If it wasn't so tragic, it would be hysterical.

'Which you'd prefer not to answer.'

'Got it in one.'

His mouth curved into a slight smile. 'Are you done?'

She borrowed his words without compunction. 'For now.'

'Let's make the most of the few hours before dawn, hmm?'

For a brief few seconds her eyes held uncertainty, followed by a degree of wariness.

'To sleep,' he added with a tinge of amusement before settling onto his back, and he proceeded to do just that within a very short period of time.

Much to her relief.

Or, so she told herself as she deliberately banished the slow-curling desire insidiously invading her body.

CHAPTER THREE

KAYLA came awake to morning sunshine filtering through the curtains and the knowledge that she was alone in the vast bed.

A quick glance at the time, and she hit the floor running.

The hospital… She'd promised Jacob she'd be there before he went in for surgery. Forget breakfast, she decided as she took care of bathroom necessities…she'd grab something later.

Clothes…jeans, a singlet top, jacket. Hair caught into a practised knot and secured with a large clip, minimal make-up, lipstick…and she emerged into the bedroom to see Duardo in the process of adjusting his tie.

Well-groomed, attired in impeccable tailoring, he looked every inch the executive entrepreneur. And far too ruggedly attractive for any woman's peace of mind.

Especially hers.

'You should have woken me.' The words were almost an accusation.

'What happened to *good morning*?' His New-York-accented drawl held indolent amusement, and she threw him a heated glance.

'Thanks to you, I'm going to be late.'

'Maria has breakfast ready for you.'

'I don't—'

'I've already phoned the hospital. Jacob won't be transferred down to Theatre until nine.'

'—have time to eat,' she concluded.

'Yes, you will.' He subjected her to a raking appraisal, noting the fine bone structure, a slenderness that was almost too lean. How many meals had she missed in the past? 'Spence will drive you there.'

She opened her mouth to protest, then closed it again.

His expression remained unchanged. 'It's his job description.' Only part of it. He extracted a cellphone from his jacket pocket and handed it to her. 'Yours. The essential numbers are already programmed in on speed-dial.'

Kayla thrust it into her shoulder bag, and looked in silent askance as he withdrew a sheaf of papers.

'Your signature is required on the marriage-licence application.'

Duardo handed her a pen, indicated where she should sign, then handed her a legal document. 'A copy of the pre-nuptial agreement for you to read. You have an appointment with my lawyer at midday to sign the original.'

Oh, my. She felt her stomach twist into a painful knot. All legalities taken care of. Somehow she didn't feel inclined to thank him.

Calm, she had to remain calm. 'I imagine you've arranged a date for this marriage?'

'Tomorrow. A Celebrant will conduct the ceremony here at the house.'

'Tomorrow.' She swallowed the sudden lump that had formed in her throat.

He withdrew his wallet, extracted several notes and handed them to her. 'I'll organize a bank account and charge-card in your name this morning. Spence will ensure you tend to the necessary paperwork.'

'You're not afraid I might abscond?' The query emerged with more flippancy than she intended, and his gaze narrowed fractionally.

'Be warned, you wouldn't get far.'

A chill settled deep in her bones. 'I made a deal,' she voiced quietly. 'There's too much at stake for me not to honour it.'

Duardo collected his briefcase in one hand and picked up his laptop. 'I'll see you tonight.'

'Late,' Kayla qualified, and at his raised eyebrow she added in explanation, 'Jacob. Hospital.'

'Spence will drop you there this afternoon.'

'I can use public transport.'

'But you won't.' There was an underlying hint of steel apparent, which she chose to ignore.

'Why not?' Besides, she wanted some degree of independence.

His eyes seared hers. 'You want to draw battle lines?'

Her head tilted a little as she held his gaze. 'Yes.'

'We'll discuss issues over dinner.'

'Let's do that.' Without a further word she made her way downstairs, aware he descended them at her side, and she didn't so much as spare him a glance as they reached the foyer and went in different directions.

Kayla found the informal dining room, and greeted the hovering Maria with a smile.

Orange juice, coffee, cereal, fruit, eggs benedict…it was a veritable feast. Her appetite, which had taken a dive, was sufficiently tempted to have a little of each.

For years, breakfast had been a gulp-and-go affair as she inevitably raced to meet the train. To sit down and

savour food without the immediate need to rush proved
something of a rarity.

Spence appeared as she drained the last of her coffee,
and she grabbed her bag and followed him out to the
four-wheel-drive.

They struck peak-hour traffic, which slowed their
progress down, and although she had a host of questions,
she asked only one. 'Did you know Duardo in New York?'

An easy smile parted his mouth. 'For a number of years.
When I expressed a desire to move to Australia, he suggested I take care of security for him.'

Had they worked the streets together and kept one step
ahead of the law? Moved on and up by the skin of their
teeth and sheer luck before exchanging the shady deals
for legitimate ones? Taking risks no sensible person
would touch, gambling both life and limb in the driven
desire to succeed?

That Duardo Alvarez had reached the pinnacle of success was no mean feat.

'Ensuring his life runs smoothly.' It was a statement, not
a query, and Spence chuckled.

'I guess you could say that.'

Security covered a whole range of possibilities, of
which bodyguard and driver were only two.

It was almost eight-thirty when Spence drew the four-
wheel-drive into the hospital's main entrance. 'Meet me
here in three quarters of an hour. Duardo suggested we un-
dertake a shopping expedition until your midday appointment with the lawyer.'

Shopping? *We*? 'You're joking, right?'

His gaze remained steady. 'You have a problem with
me accompanying you?'

Oh, my. 'Not if you're authorised to use Duardo's credit

card.' Kayla checked her watch, then offered a dazzling smile. 'Nine-fifteen.'

It took only minutes to reach the upper floor and locate Jacob's room, a single suite with a view from the window.

'Hi.' Kayla crossed to the bed and brushed her lips to his forehead.

'Right back at you.'

His voice was drowsy with the faint huskiness of sedation, and her heart ached for him.

He was all she had. The one person who'd been there for her, unconditionally, since their mother's death.

Together they'd shared the grief, weathered the despair and fought to regain a modicum of dignity through Benjamin's fall from grace.

And afterwards, when the grim reality of poverty made itself felt, Jacob had given up everything...as she had...to work every waking hour in an effort to survive.

She noted the bruises to his jaw, his cheek...much more noticeable than they had been last night. How many more were there, marring his young body?

His leg...his shattered knee. It sickened her to think of the surgery he had to undergo, and she worried if it would be totally successful. If he'd be left with a limp...not be able to run or play sport.

His welfare brought vividly to mind just what Duardo's proposition meant in *real* terms. And why she'd accepted it.

'How are you feeling?'

A faint smile parted his lips. 'Almost out of it.'

'You're going to be fine.' Words, sincerely meant in reassurance.

He squeezed her hand. 'Thanks.'

Tears momentarily blurred her vision, and she blinked rapidly to dispel them.

Within minutes a nurse appeared, took his vital signs, then signalled for an Orderly to take the patient to Theatre.

'There's a visitors' lounge at the end of the corridor where you can wait. A cafeteria on the next level.' She checked her watch. 'Given surgery, recovery, he won't be back in his room much under five hours.'

Jacob managed a slow smile as the Orderly trundled the bed from the suite, and Kayla walked at his side until they reached the lift.

She left her cellphone number with the sister-in-charge, together with a request to call should Jacob recover from the anaesthetic sooner than anticipated.

Spence was waiting when she emerged from the main entrance, and his choice of venues soon became apparent when he entered Double Bay.

Exclusive *expensive* boutiques, and once, in another life, her preferred shopping mecca. An area where serious money could be spent on designer originals…apparel, shoes, bags, jewellery.

'Wedding attire is a priority,' Spence informed as they hit the pavement.

Was she supposed to display joyous anticipation? Enthusiasm? Just how much did Spence know of her connection with his boss?

Enough. It couldn't be any other way.

'You'll need to enlighten me.'

He didn't pretend to misunderstand. 'A small, intimate ceremony, with myself and Duardo's lawyer as witnesses.'

No guests. Well, that narrowed it down. 'Classy, but not over-the-top.' And not *bridal.* She could do that.

Elegant boho-chic, white or cream, stilettos, a single,

long-stemmed red rose held in one hand? Too fashionable-of-the-moment?

Maybe she should go for formal black, or deep scarlet. Although she doubted Duardo would appreciate or approve of the irony.

She found the perfect outfit in the first boutique she entered. In pale cream, it was a nineteen-twenties-style dress with a delicate crystal-beaded skirt overlay reaching just below her knees, and a sleeveless beaded top. It was elegant, outlined her slender curves, and felt *right*.

Different, so very different from the long white fitted gown she'd packed to take to Hawaii for her first wedding.

Then she'd married for love, and had melted into Duardo's bed with willing fervour.

Now…now it seemed as if a hundred butterflies had taken up residence in her stomach at the mere thought.

Could she slip easily into intimacy? Close her eyes and pretend? Enjoy what they'd once shared together?

The vivid memory of how it had been heated her blood and caused sensation to pool deep inside.

Don't *think*, a silent voice bade. Just…deal with it.

Kayla took a deep breath and spared her mirrored image another critical look. Yes. The dress more than met the required criteria for a quiet civil ceremony.

The price tag sent her into a momentary state of shock. So, too, did the matching stilettos.

How times had changed. Five years ago she wouldn't have given the cost a second thought. Now she stood to one side while Spence presented Duardo's credit card and the boutique *vendeuse* packaged the purchases.

She spared the lingerie boutique a quick glance and walked on by…only to pause when Spence redirected her inside.

It was akin to being shown Aladdin's cave. Exquisite silk and lace in abundance. She could have had a field-day. Instead she selected a matching bra and brief set, and ignored Spence's encouragement to add more to a steadily growing collection of glossy carrier-bags.

There was time for a restorative coffee before dealing with the bank, the lawyer to sign the pre-nuptial agreement…whereupon she was handed a manila envelope.

'Duardo instructed me to give you these copies.'

For a moment she looked startled, then realisation hit. Documented proof of Duardo's takeover bid of Benjamin's company.

It was after two when Spence drew the four-wheel-drive to a halt outside the hospital entrance.

'I'll take the shopping home and have Maria put it in your room.'

'Thanks.' Kayla reached for the door clasp. 'And thanks for today. I appreciated your help.'

His smile held genuine warmth. 'You're welcome.'

Jacob's suite was empty when she reached it, and she sought out the sister-in-charge, who, on enquiry, relayed the reconstructive surgery had taken longer than anticipated and it could be another hour before Jacob was returned to the ward.

The cafeteria seemed a good choice, and she filled in time with a cool drink whilst leafing through a few complimentary magazines.

Although her mind kept wandering as she reflected on the day…and wondered what the night would bring.

Get a grip. It wasn't as if she hadn't been to bed with him before. Dammit, she'd lain at his side through last night…and woken with the knowledge he only had to make the slightest move for her to go into meltdown.

It didn't make sense. The mind and body should be in sync…yet hers seemed to be two separate entities with different agendas.

Speaking of which, there was one glaring error in her purchases, and she went in search of the medical centre, secured a prescription for the contraceptive pill then sought out the pharmacy dispensary.

Jacob had just been trundled into his suite when she entered it, and she stood to one side as the Orderly and nurse tended to routine.

'Your brother is heavily sedated and on pain relief,' the nurse informed. 'He'll be very drowsy for some time.'

An understatement, for over the next few hours he stirred momentarily, acknowledged where he was, smiled at her then he lapsed back to sleep.

A nurse checked him on the hour. 'I think it would be wise for you to go home and visit tomorrow,' she advised kindly.

'An excellent idea,' a familiar male voice drawled from the doorway.

Duardo, Kayla perceived, aware of the forceful image he presented as he entered the suite. His eyes were dark and faintly hooded as they met her own.

'I've spoken with the surgeon. The reconstruction has been successful. He endorsed the level of Jacob's sedation and pain control.'

She was reluctant to leave, and said so. 'Visiting hours aren't over yet.'

'It's doubtful Jacob will do more than stir through the night.'

Two against one. Common sense won out, and she addressed the nurse as she stood. 'Please make sure he knows I was here.'

'Of course.'

Kayla exited the ward at Duardo's side, and rode the lift down to ground level in silence, waiting until they reached his Aston Martin before offering, 'There was no need for you to come collect me.'

'We've already done this.'

She sent him a dark glance which lost much of its impact in the dim night light. 'Thoughtfulness and consideration, Duardo?' She waited a beat. 'Or taking care of a debt owed in human form?'

'Get in the car, Kayla.' His voice held a dangerous silkiness. 'And curb your acerbic tongue.'

'Is that a threat?'

'Open to interpretation.'

She had to be insane to best him. It simply wouldn't happen…unless he allowed it. And that was about as likely as a cow jumping over the moon!

Kayla slid into the passenger seat and secured the safety belt as he set the car in motion.

She chose silence as they traversed the suburban streets, and her nerves frayed a little as Duardo entered Double Bay. An area where some of the city's social echelon elected to dine in exclusive restaurants favoured for their boutique cuisine. If you wanted to be *seen*, this was the place.

'I'm not very hungry.' She became very conscious of her attire…jeans and a jacket didn't really cut it.

He slid into a parking space and switched off the engine. 'We both need to eat.' He spared her a sweeping glance. 'And you're fine as you are.'

She had one advantage, she decided minutes later as the *maître d'* greeted him with obsequious beneficence and promptly found them a table. She was with Duardo Alvarez…and that, she perceived wryly, said it all.

She declined wine, selected a starter as a main with fresh fruit to follow, while Duardo ordered an exotic seafood pilaf.

'You mentioned issues,' Kayla began. 'Shall we discuss them?'

Duardo shot her a faintly musing look. 'Let's eat first, hmm?'

She could do polite...she'd had years of practice. 'I should thank you for Spence's services today.' And gratitude, where it was due. 'We shopped.'

'At my instigation.' He sank back in his chair. 'You object?'

'What woman would?' she parried lightly.

The waiter brought their meal, and she forked small morsels of food from the decoratively arranged plate, extremely conscious of her surroundings and fellow patrons.

Duardo Alvarez bore instant recognition, and without doubt there was covert speculation as to her identity. Something that would intensify as her position in his life became known.

Sordid details would resurface and be rehashed by the gossip-mongers, creating an emotional storm she'd be forced to weather beneath the glare of publicity.

OK, so she'd get to smile a lot and play *pretend*.

'You're very quiet.'

Kayla pushed her plate to one side and took a sip of iced water. 'You want scintillating conversation, Duardo?'

'Not particularly.' It was a pleasant change to sit opposite a woman and not have her indulge in the flirting game. The subtle and often not-so-subtle prelude to an invitation to her bed.

'Then perhaps we should move along to the issues we need to discuss.'

He viewed her with speculative amusement. 'You have a list?'

'And you don't?'

The waiter delivered a platter of artistically displayed fresh fruit, and took their orders for coffee.

'You have household staff who run your home like clockwork,' Kayla ventured. 'I'd like to resume working. Part-time, flexi-time.' When this was greeted with silence, she continued, 'I need to know where Jacob will convalesce.' Oh, why not go for broke? 'I don't want—'

'Duardo! *Amico.*'

Duardo rose to his feet and took the man's extended hand. An older man, in his mid- to late-fifties, with a young woman at his side.

With accustomed ease Duardo effected an introduction. 'Darling…Benito Torres and his wife, Samara.'

Darling?

Benito's smile held musing indulgence as he indicated Kayla. 'And this charming young lady is?'

'Soon to become my wife.'

Was it her imagination or did Samara's eyes harden a little?

'However did you manage to get Duardo to put a ring on your finger?' The woman's voice held warm amusement, but there was something in the tone that didn't quite match up.

'By refusing to sleep with him.' There, make of that what you will!

Samara gave a disbelieving laugh. 'How…quaintly old-fashioned.' She pressed a brightly lacquered fingernail against Duardo's forearm and fluttered heavily mascaraed lashes at him. 'And…risky, surely?'

'He's taken, *querida*,' Benito drawled. 'And he doesn't share.'

'Shame.'

The coy seductiveness was a mite overdone, and Kayla viewed their departure with interest.

'A past lover?'

Duardo's gaze remained level. 'No.'

The truth? Did it matter?

She told herself she didn't care…and knew she lied.

The waiter brought their coffee, and she took hers black with sugar, aware he matched her actions.

'We were discussing issues,' Kayla ventured. Before the interruption of Benito Torres and his wife.

'I gather you don't want to be a social butterfly, filling your days with luncheons, charity functions, shopping and personal maintenance?'

'Not particularly.'

'You no longer have cause to work.'

She sipped her coffee, savoured the rich caffeine then carefully replaced her cup onto its saucer. 'Don't you get it?' Her eyes sparked with brilliant blue fire. 'I don't want to be beholden to you for every cent I need!'

Duardo sank back in his chair and regarded her with speculative interest. 'You'll have a monthly allowance.'

Her anger didn't diminish. 'A *clothing* allowance,' she agreed, aware she'd never be able to afford the designer gear worn by the city's fashionistas who formed part of Duardo's social circle.

'Jacob—'

'Will move into an apartment when he leaves hospital.'

'What apartment? Where?' She'd thought, *hoped* Jacob would convalesce in Duardo's home. Dammit, the house was big enough to accommodate several guests.

'Rose Bay.'

'Don't tell me. You own it.'

'The building,' he illuminated in dry, mocking tones.

'He'll need care, physiotherapy—'

'Which he'll have. Until he's fully mobile, Spence will transport Jacob wherever he needs to go.' Duardo finished his coffee.

'Divide and conquer, Duardo?'

He regarded her thoughtfully. 'Your brother has the opportunity to lead his own life. I suggest you allow him to do so.'

'When he's fully recovered,' Kayla qualified, and met the lurking cynicism in those dark eyes.

He signalled the waiter, requested and paid the bill. 'Are you done?'

'No,' she managed sweetly as she rose to her feet and preceded him from the restaurant.

The close confines of the Aston Martin made her acutely aware of his presence…and the slow burn of heat filling her body.

It shouldn't *be* like this. Dammit, she didn't *want* to feel this way. Nor did she want to be sexually possessed by him.

She'd been there, briefly, and had never fully recovered from the encounter. In those few halcyon days of marriage he'd taught her so much…too much, she reflected as the car traversed the short distance to Point Piper.

It had made her want only *him*. The mesmeric, electrifying ecstasy…wild, driven need in its most primitive form. But it was more than primeval coupling…sensual magic, where two minds, two bodies were in perfect accord, each the other half of a whole.

The whole deal. Not just sex.

Get a grip, why don't you?

That was the past.

Now, through circumstance, she had no recourse but to forge some form of future with Duardo Alvarez.

Live with him, lie with him.

A slight shiver feathered its way down her spine.

She hadn't escaped emotionally unscathed from the divorce. How could she hope to survive in a loveless marriage?

Kayla became conscious of the sudden silence, and realized the car was stationary in the garage.

A large area housing two late-model four-wheel-drive vehicles. A gold Lexus and dark blue BMW.

With slightly shaky fingers she released the seat belt and slid out of the car.

Duardo loosened his tie as they hit the lobby, and she watched as he shrugged out of his suit jacket and hooked it over one shoulder.

'I need to access emails and make a few international calls.'

'OK.' Kayla made for the stairs, and on reaching their suite she shed her clothes and headed for the shower. When she was done she pulled on a towelling robe and checked out the television console in the adjoining bedroom alcove.

She channel-surfed, settled on an episode of *Law & Order* and curled up in one of the comfortable leather sofas.

It was there Duardo found her, asleep, with her head nestled against the arm of the sofa, her hair spilling free like a curtain of pale silk.

For several minutes he stood observing the steady rise and fall of her breathing, aware of her fragility, her latent strength.

A contradiction in terms.

She felt light in his arms. Too light, he determined as

he moved towards the bed, and his grasp tightened as she began to stir, then came fully awake.

'What are you doing?' A half-hearted query, if ever there was one. She had instant recall of viewing TV...then blissful oblivion.

'Taking you to bed.'

'No.' Too late—they were already there. 'Please.' Her face was only inches from his, and she became aware of the gaping edges of her towelling robe...the fact he'd showered and pulled on a robe of his own. 'Put me down.'

Duardo complied, his eyes narrowing at the flood of pink tingeing her cheeks as she quickly fixed her robe and put some distance between them.

He looked strong, *vital*, and far too disturbingly male for any woman's peace of mind. Especially hers!

Sensation spiralled deep inside, meshing sensual heat with unwanted desire as she recalled all too vividly what it felt like to have him touch her.

The light brush of his mouth against each sensitive pulse-beat, the curve of her breast and the sensual pull of his tongue as it laved its peak.

How he had adored to explore her body, and gift her the most intimate kiss of all, driving her wild until she begged like a craven wanton for release...savouring her climax, before sending her to the brink again, holding her there, then plunging deep to take her with him.

Sensual sexual magic so incredibly exquisite it almost defied description.

For those beautiful few days, she had loved with her heart and soul...and believed herself loved in return.

Fool. Days were all she'd had before the bubble burst.

Now *love* no longer existed, and what they'd once shared could never be resurrected.

It gave her the nerve to voice the words tumbling around inside her head. Get it over and done with. Now.

'I want you to wear protection when we have sex.'

His expression didn't change, although she had the distinct impression there was anger lurking beneath the surface of his control. 'Your reason being?'

Her eyes met and held his with fearless disregard. 'I don't think it's fair to have an unplanned pregnancy.'

'Have I asked you to have my child?'

'No.' It was impossible not to visualize a boy infant in his father's image: a strong, forceful, dark-haired imp.

'You're concerned about health issues?'

'Not on my part.' That came out too quickly, and his eyes narrowed.

'You think I may have disregarded the wisdom of safe sex?'

The thought of him being with other women, indulging, sharing the sensual delights he'd gifted *her* was almost more than she could bear. 'I doubt you've remained celibate during the past three years.'

Brave fool. He wanted to shake her. 'And you, Kayla?' His voice was as silk-smooth and held a dangerous edge.

Damn him. There was no way she'd give him satisfaction of the truth. 'Our divorce absolved us from the vow of fidelity.'

'That doesn't answer the question.'

She met his gaze and held it. 'It's one you don't have the right to ask.'

Duardo took a step towards her, and she stood her ground despite every instinct warning her to turn and run.

'There's something else,' she continued, ignoring the muscle bunching at the edge of his jaw. 'Blood tests.'

Pushing him to the edge was the height of folly. Yet she was besieged with a host of emotions, not the least of which was a volatile mix of anger and desire.

She didn't want him. Couldn't need him. Yet the dictates of her body warred with rationale…and she hated him for it. Most of all, she hated herself.

'My word is insufficient?'

Was it? She no longer knew.

When she didn't answer, he crossed to a bedside pedestal, withdrew a slip of paper and handed it to her.

It took only seconds to scan the pathology report.

Should she thank, or condemn him?

Neither, she decided, hating that he was light-years ahead of her.

'That takes care of all the issues?'

His voice was deceptively mild, and she controlled the faint shiver threatening to slither down her spine.

'For the moment.'

'Good.' He reached out a hand and slid his fingers through her hair, holding fast her nape as he angled his head and closed his mouth over hers.

Evocative, intensely sensual, he played her with shameless ease, tasting the soft inner tissues, probing her tongue with his own, teasing, until a silent groan rose in her throat.

Kayla clenched a hand and aimed it at his shoulder, with no effect whatsoever.

Their bodies weren't even touching, yet it felt as if she was being absorbed by him, with any resistance fading into insignificance.

He knew how to please, with an eroticism that swept away any clarity of thought until there was only the moment, the man and the need to respond.

It would be so easy to slide the robe off his shoulders, shuck aside her own and lean into him.

Skin on skin, to taste and pleasure him, seductively explore until he lost his breath, his mind.

Except she did none of those things, and the breath caught in her throat as he loosened her robe and slid a hand to cup her breast, then tantalise its peak.

She closed her eyes, successfully veiling their expression as he trailed an unerring path to its twin, caught the hardened bud between thumb and forefinger and rolled it gently until she fought back an inaudible groan.

His hand slid to her navel, lingered there, then trailed over her trembling belly, seeking her sensitive clitoris in an intimate exploration that sent her high on a tide of exquisite sensation so acute she sank into him.

His mouth left hers and settled at the edge of her throat, savoured the delicate hollow and absorbed the vibration as she held back a silent scream.

It was almost more than she could bear as he urged her to the brink again, kept her there then held her as tiny shockwaves shook her body.

With slow, deliberate movements he put her at arm's length, then traced gentle fingers over her slightly swollen mouth.

'I hate you.' It came out as a husky whisper, and her lips trembled beneath his touch. Her eyes were large blue limpid pools, and he watched as moisture welled and threatened to spill.

'At this precise moment, I imagine you do.' He tucked wayward strands of hair back behind each ear, then let his hand slide down her jaw to cup her chin. 'And hate yourself even more.'

He dropped his hand and crossed round to the other side

of the bed, shed his robe and slid in between the sheets. In one easy movement he snapped off the bedside lamp, plunging the room into shadowy darkness.

Kayla wanted to throw something at him, and caught up a pillow ready to hurl at his hapless head.

Strong fingers closed over her wrist. 'Don't even think about it.'

The air between them was electric, yet she was too angry to take much heed as she attempted to wrench her hand free. 'Let me go.'

'Drop the pillow.'

'Like hell.'

In one fluid movement Duardo dispensed of the pillow with one hand and exerted sufficient leverage to tumble her down on top of him.

'Don't.' The word escaped as a helplessly torn plea an instant before his mouth took possession of her own.

This was no exploratory dance. Intense, hungry, it became a prelude to more, so much more than she wanted him to take.

She was barely conscious of movement as he reversed their positions, until he began tracing a path to her breast, savoured one, moved to tease the tender peak, then travelled low to seek the sensitive core at the apex of her thighs.

Oh, dear God.

She didn't want him there. Didn't want the primitive ecstasy his touch would bring...or his possession.

Because then she'd be lost. Driven by a hunger so acute, she'd no longer belong to herself...but to him. Spiritually, emotionally, physically...*his*.

Liquid fire ran through her body, heating it to fever pitch as he bestowed primeval pleasure so intense she cried out, tossing her head from side to side in a puny attempt at control.

Except she had none.

He made sure of it, and when he eased into her he covered her mouth with his own, swallowing her faint cries as her inner muscles stretched and began to convulse as she accommodated him.

He held himself there for timeless seconds, then he began to move...slowly at first, coaxing her to match his rhythm until they were in sync.

Driven wild, it was she who rose up against him, taking him even deeper inside. She who reversed their positions in a need to ride him hard, fast...until everything splintered in tumultuous climax.

Tears of emotion welled in her eyes and she held them back with sheer effort of will. The temptation to cry was almost more than she could bear, and a silent sob shook her slim form as Duardo traced the contours of each breast, focusing on the swollen peaks rendered tender from his mouth, the edges of his teeth.

Her throat convulsed, and she attempted to swallow the sudden lump that had formed there.

She was still joined with him, exulting in his possession, the feel of him, the musky heat of his body, her own, as her heartbeat slowed to a normal rhythm.

A single tear hung suspended at the edge of her jaw, then fell, and she heard his soft oath, felt the tips of his fingers trace her cheeks, discover the wet rivulets.

Then he drew her down against him and cushioned her head into the curve of his shoulder.

She felt his lips brush her forehead, felt him pull the bedcovers up over them both and felt a hand settle at her nape while the other soothed a path along her spine.

What they'd shared, she reflected tremulously, had been all about her.

Her pleasure, her climax.

'Go to sleep.'

Sure. As if that would happen any time soon.

Except she did slip into blissful oblivion, eventually, long after his breathing steadied.

CHAPTER FOUR

KAYLA stretched languidly, felt the pull of unused muscles, the lingering sensation of fairly vigorous sex and closed her eyes against the flood of memories filling her mind.

Dammit, she could still *feel* him inside her. His imprint, the touch of his mouth, his hands.

The sexual heat, the witching, incredibly sensuous *sex*.

For that was all it had been. A physical coupling of two people sexually in tune with each other.

Sure. Who was she trying to kid?

Rise and shine, shower, dress and face the day, she commanded silently as she slid quickly from the bed and made for the *en suite*.

Cargo pants, a cotton singlet top, heeled sandals, her hair caught in a low pony-tail, she made her way down to the breakfast room...and discovered Duardo had already left for the city.

'Shopping,' Spence informed as he entered the room just as she finished her coffee.

'You're kidding. Again?'

He inclined his head. 'Duardo's instructions.'

Well, then...who was she to argue? 'And visit Jacob,' she added as she rose to her feet.

'We need to be home no later than three. The ceremony is scheduled at five.'

The *wedding*.

Dear heaven. By the end of the day she'd be Kayla Antonia *Alvarez*.

For the second time.

'Of course.' Was that her voice? It sounded calm, when inside she was rapidly becoming a nervous wreck.

Something which didn't diminish as the day progressed.

If anything, it became worse...so much so, she could barely eat, as each morsel seemed to stick in her throat.

It didn't help that Jacob was heavily sedated with pain management, and kept lapsing into drug-induced silence.

All day she'd alternated between running off at the mouth with seemingly inane conversation, and lapsing into silence.

She needed support. Yet there was no one to call on. Not even the man who was soon to become her husband.

Their wedding wasn't sufficiently important for him to make any concession other than to indicate, via Spence, to expect him home earlier than usual.

She'd never felt so alone in her life.

Everything was laid out on the bed in readiness, and she thanked Maria for her kind attention.

'I've put everything away, except this.' The housekeeper picked up a large envelope. 'It was in one of the bags. It has your name on it.'

A slight frown creased Kayla's forehead an instant before comprehension hit.

The legal paperwork Duardo's lawyer had been instructed to hand her...documenting proof of the takeover bid.

Kayla slit open the flap and extracted the document.

Dates. She didn't need to read the legalese. Nevertheless, she skimmed it just the same.

And felt her stomach execute a slow somersault as it became shockingly aware Benjamin had lied to her.

She closed her eyes, then opened them again.

If her father had lied about this…what other lies had he fed her?

How could he? To have gone to these lengths… Her mind whirled at the implications.

Dear heaven.

Somehow she had to gather her shattered thoughts, for in a little more than an hour she was due to get married. And she needed to shower, fix her hair, apply make-up…and dress.

It was almost four-thirty when she stepped into the cream beaded dress, and reached for the zip fastening.

'Let me help with that,' Duardo drawled, and his fingers brushed hers as he slid the fastener home.

He had the tread of a cat, for she hadn't heard him enter the room.

He turned her around to face him, and his eyes narrowed at the sight of her pale features, the large sapphire-blue pools' dilation depicted some of her inner stress.

Don't…offer platitudes, or touch me, she silently begged, feeling utterly fragile. If he did either, she'd splinter into a thousand pieces at his feet.

'Give me twenty minutes to shower, shave and dress, then we'll go downstairs together.'

There was never going to be a right time…but she needed to say the words. 'I owe you an apology.'

He stilled, and she rushed into speech. 'The takeover bid. Dates. My father lied.' Oh, God, she was a trembling mess. 'I'm sorry.'

'Apology accepted,' he said quietly, then shrugged out of his jacket, dispensed with his shoes and disappeared into his *en suite*.

He made it in nineteen…sheer nervousness ensured she'd checked almost every passing minute.

Spence, Maria and Josef, together with the Celebrant, were waiting for them in the formal lounge. A small linen-covered table was set with a beautiful display of roses, and a candle sat waiting to be lit.

Introductions complete, the Celebrant intoned the necessary words that legally bound Kayla and Duardo together as husband and wife.

The exchange of rings completed the ceremony, and she felt the breath catch in her throat as he slid the wide diamond-encrusted band on her finger, for it was the original ring he'd gifted her to seal their first marriage. So, too, was the wide gold diamond-studded band she was handed to slip onto his finger.

He'd kept them?

Why?

Duardo lowered his head and lightly brushed his lips against her own. In that instant her eyes fused with his, their expression naked for a few timeless seconds in the intense desire to glimpse anything in his expression that would give hint their spoken vows held meaning. That the passion they'd shared through the night was more than just…very good sex.

Even now, she still carried the sensual awareness of sexual possession. The instinctive flare of arousal as the mind provided a tellingly vivid image.

He knew. She could tell by the slumberous gleam in those dark eyes, so close to her own.

Was it male satisfaction at reclaiming her as his wife? Or

the culmination of revenge? Sadly, she suspected it was both.

Together they lit the candle, signed the marriage certificate and thanked the Celebrant.

Spence presented a bottle of Cristal champagne, filled crystal flutes and made a toast, while Maria produced a tray of canapés.

Within what seemed to be a fairly short space of time the Celebrant took her leave, Maria and Josef made a discreet exit, followed by Spence.

'I've made a booking for dinner at seven.' Duardo took the empty flute from her fingers and placed it with his own on a nearby chiffonier.

Dinner? They were eating out? Again?

'A personal celebration.'

It was certainly personal. But hardly a celebration, she determined as she ascended the stairs to freshen up.

Although, on second thoughts, she preferred being in the company of others to an intimate meal *á deux* at home.

There was a matching evening purse that came with the dress, and she quickly popped in lipstick, tissues and a folded note.

Money, darling, she could almost hear her late mother's words in musing wisdom. *Never go anywhere without it. Especially in the company of a man*.

Mad money. Taxi money, Kayla reflected as she retreated downstairs.

The Aston Martin was Duardo's chosen method of transport for the night, their destination the exclusive Ritz Carlton at Double Bay, whose exemplary restaurant was high on the list of *places to be seen*.

Was that his intention?

The *maître d'* led them to a secluded table, Duardo

conferred with the drinks steward and, after perusing the menu, they placed their order.

Exquisite food, artistically presented, accompanied by a fine wine…

Beautiful, elegantly attired patrons willing to pay the price to portray a given façade.

Somehow it was difficult to see Duardo buying into it. Yet to him it was a game, an ongoing challenge, to be perceived as the man he had become. Proof that wealth could conquer almost anything.

Yet the core of the youth he had been in the tough streets of New York remained buried deep beneath the acquired sophisticated image.

It was evident in the hardness of his eyes, the leashed savagery apparent in the frightening stillness of his body.

She'd witnessed it three years ago when she'd chosen family and handed back his ring.

Control…he had it. But the hidden threat remained.

'Have I suddenly grown horns?'

Duardo's drawl held faint mockery, and she met his steady gaze with equanimity. 'The jury is still out.'

His soft chuckle curled round her nerve-ends and tugged a little. 'And not about to reach a decision any time soon.'

'No.'

There was no sense of elation at re-entering the social scene, even as Duardo's wife. The prospect of needing to play *pretend* didn't thrill her at all, for the knowledge that the smiles, the bonhomie, were as fake as their marriage would merely serve as proof almost everything about her life was based on falsehood.

'Nevertheless, I suggest you practice a smile.'

'You have a reason?'

'A photographer scouting for a newsworthy shot.'

Oh, hell. 'Charming.'

'Play nice, hmm?'

'I wouldn't dream of doing otherwise,' she assured, adding, 'in public.'

Then it was photo time, and when the photographer's sidekick noticed both wedding rings there were voiced congratulations and much scribbling on a notepad.

By tomorrow, news of their remarriage would be recorded in the social pages of the city's major newspapers.

Kayla waited until the team was out of earshot. 'A deliberate orchestration, Duardo?'

'No.'

Could she believe him? Did it matter?

'It's timely,' he continued with thinly veiled mockery. 'Given we're due to appear together at a charity fundraiser tomorrow evening.'

They were?

The thought of being launched onto the social scene after a long hiatus was a trifle daunting.

'Advance information to feed or minimize the gossipmill?'

He replaced his flatware onto the plate before choosing to respond. 'I imagine it will achieve both.'

Without doubt. A ready smile curved her lips, but her eyes lacked humour. '*Wonderful.*'

'You'll cope.'

Yes, she would. But she retained vivid memories of her father's slide on the social scale. Dinners postponed, then cancelled, and invitations dwindling down to none. Longtime friends who no longer wanted to be associated with Benjamin Enright-Smythe or his daughter or son.

The experience had made her very aware that life was all about survival of self in a world where reality ruled.

Kayla took a sip of wine, and replaced the stemmed goblet with a steady hand.

A charity fund-raiser attracted the city's social echelon, where the female guests vied to outdo each other in evening gowns, jewellery, and spent the entire day in personal preparation for each event.

'I have yet to add an evening gown to my purchases.'

Duardo sank back in his chair and viewed her with veiled scrutiny. 'I suggest you take care of it tomorrow.'

'Acquiring a trophy wife could prove expensive.'

His eyes narrowed fractionally. 'If I had wanted a trophy wife, you wouldn't be here.'

The implications sent ice scudding through her veins as a mental picture flashed through her mind…new town, new identity for herself and Jacob and living in constant fear of when the loan-shark thugs would find them.

Kayla pushed her plate to one side, her appetite gone. There was nothing cognizant she could offer in response, and it was a relief when the waiter delivered coffee prior to Duardo settling the bill.

It wasn't late when they exited the restaurant, and as the car whispered almost soundlessly through the streets it was impossible not to recall her first wedding night. A meal where they had fed each other morsels of food and were oblivious to everything and everyone. How they'd walked barefoot along the white sands at Waikiki Beach, savouring each moment until they returned to their suite to make love all through the night.

Magic. The distant lap of an incoming tide, the soft sound of background music from the resident band.

She'd gifted him her body, her soul…*love*. And believed it to be reciprocated.

Nothing else had mattered then.

Until reality intervened, and she'd made the wrong choice.

Had there been any *right* choice?

Now she was back with the man who'd succeeded in stealing her heart. Except everything had changed. This time round, revenge was his motive, not love.

And *you*? a mental voice intruded. Is survival your only motive?

Are you *insane*?

Don't answer that.

Lights sprang on along the curved driveway as Duardo used the remote to open the electronic gates guarding the entrance to his home, and sensor-activated illumination lit the portico and selected interior lighting.

'Champagne? Coffee?'

Kayla's steps didn't falter as she crossed the foyer and made for the stairs. 'Neither, thanks.'

He could follow, or not. It hardly made any difference, and she didn't look back to check as she entered the master suite.

On the night of their first marriage he'd swept an arm beneath her knees and carried her into their hotel suite, fed her sweet strawberries tipped with chocolate and dipped in champagne, then slowly, with infinite care, divested her of her clothes, his own, and gently tutored her in the art of lovemaking.

Now she slipped off her stilettos, carefully removed her dress then padded into the *en suite*. It took only minutes to complete the nightly ritual, undress and slip on her robe.

When she emerged the bedroom was empty, and she crossed to the alcove, opened the television and flicked through a few channels until she found an interesting programme, then sank down into a chair to watch it.

There was little awareness of the passage of time as she became engrossed in the documentary.

'Unable to sleep?'

She gave a startled gasp and turned to face him, unaware he'd entered the room or exchanged clothes for his robe. 'How long have you been here?'

'Only minutes.' He scooped her into his arms in one fluid movement, then sank down in the chair with her on his lap.

'What do you think you're doing?' She attempted to struggle free, and failed miserably.

He curved a hand over her shoulder and edged her close in against his chest. 'You need me to answer that?'

She felt the warmth of his palm as it slid beneath her robe, cupped her breast and rested there.

Her heartbeat picked up, and she silently damned the effect he roused in her. Worse, that he couldn't fail to be aware of it.

How easy would it be to lift her face to his and nuzzle her lips to his throat, then seek his mouth with her own? To indulge each other with an exploratory tasting…

Fool.

The past and the present didn't mesh. First time round, love had had everything to do with it. Now it didn't form part of the equation.

To sit here quiescent was impossible, and she caught hold of his wrist in an attempt to pull free. Without success.

'Let me up.'

'Uncomfortable?'

Brilliant blue eyes stormed his. 'Don't play me.'

'You think this is a game?'

The anger intensified. 'Yes!' And she added a silent *damn you.*

He caught hold of her chin and tilted it, then his mouth captured her own in a kiss that plundered with devastating effect and stilled any protest she tried to voice.

Kayla balled one hand into a fist and aimed a wild punch that found no purchase.

His mouth lifted briefly, then resettled to conduct a frankly sensual invasion...tormenting, caressing without surcease until she gave in with an almost inaudible groan and began to respond.

It wasn't until she felt the mattress beneath her back that she realized he'd moved to the bed, and she stilled for a few timeless seconds before giving in to the heat, the passion, exulting in his touch and her own rapturous response.

The desire to test his control and have him lose it was impossible to resist, and she waited until he was on the edge of sleep before initiating an evocative exploration of her own.

With fingers as light as a butterfly's touch she traced the compacted muscles above his stomach, felt the reactive flex, then trailed to one male nipple and gently rolled it between thumb and forefinger before scraping it lightly with a lacquered nail.

She found the indentation of his navel, teased its outline and delved into its centre before trailing a slow path to sink fingers into the pubic hair couching his penis. Caught his faint intake of breath and felt his erection.

A fascinating part of the male anatomy...such strength and flexibility. An instrument able to bestow such pleasure. Sensitive to the slightest touch.

A secret smile curved her lips, only to freeze as strong fingers closed over her wrist. 'I suggest you stop right there.'

Revenge, such as it was, felt so darned *good*. '*Darling*.' The word slipped from her tongue with droll mockery, in deliberate payback. 'I've barely begun.' She paused almost imperceptibly. 'Too much for you to handle?'

A faint sound emerged from his throat…a subdued groan, or stifled laughter?

She told herself she didn't care.

He released her hand. 'Be aware it can have only one end.'

It became an endurance test…his, as she teased and tantalized, with her hands, the edge of her tongue, the gentle nip of her teeth. A delicate salutation that caused male fingers tracing the length of her spine to dig in as if in silent warning.

An action that had her cup his scrotum and squeeze a little, before tracing the swollen, distended length of his erection with the tip of her finger, circle its head, then tease with unrelenting fervour.

'Enough.'

Duardo reversed their positions and surged deep inside her with one powerful thrust, unleashing an erotic, primeval coupling that became wild as they drove each other to the limit, suspended themselves there, then sent each other spiralling in a glorious free fall.

Had she cried out? There was no recollection of anything other than the witching sorcery of incredible sex and its aftermath.

The long, slow slide of his hand traced the contours of her body, and she felt the brush of his lips to her temple.

She didn't want to move. Didn't think she *could*.

A husky protest escaped her lips as strong arms slid beneath her body, carried her into the *en suite* and joined her in a spa bath filled with warm scented water.

She didn't bother opening her eyes. 'This is a dream, right?'

'Uh-huh.'

The water felt good, so, too, the leisurely ministrations, the soft towel blotting moisture from her body, the comfortable mattress, the bedcovers.

And the arms that held her as she slept.

'Rise and shine. It's after ten.'

Kayla heard the words, and burrowed her head beneath the pillow. Only to groan out loud as the pillow was removed.

'Doesn't rhyme,' she muttered. 'Should be nine.'

'Ten,' a familiar male voice corrected, and she rolled over to face her nemesis. Only to close her eyes and open them again.

He looked too rested, too relaxed and too darn *male*.

'Breakfast,' Duardo drawled. 'Followed by some retail therapy.'

She lifted a hand and smoothed back a fall of hair from her cheek. 'I'm all shopped out.'

'Tonight. Charity fund-raiser. Evening gown.'

'Oh, *hell*.'

'Just so. Except the charity is a very worthy cause, and the event is one I'm expected to attend.' He leant down and placed a hand on the bedcovers. 'Spence is waiting for you.'

So he was, she determined as she finished off a healthy breakfast and two cups of black coffee.

They visited Jacob, who appeared in good spirits, and his congratulatory hug and good wishes held genuine warmth. It was a relief to have his assurance the pain factor was manageable, and the orthopaedist pleased with his progress.

'This is becoming a habit,' Kayla imparted as Spence hit Double Bay and they entered the first of several boutiques.

By early afternoon Spence had a number of glossy carrier-bags in his possession, and there was a sense of relief they were done.

'Home,' Kayla declared as he stowed everything in the Lexus.

'Not quite.'

She looked at him in silent askance, then voiced, 'Why do I get the feeling there's *more*?'

'Lunch.'

'That's it?'

'Jewellery.' He named an exclusive boutique. 'Duardo suggests you choose from a few pieces he instructed be put aside.'

She almost refused to comply. Except she recognized the purpose. As Duardo Alvarez's wife there were certain expectations to uphold. It was everything to do with image.

An hour later she stood with Spence in locked seclusion as she examined exquisite diamonds in various settings. After some deliberation and adherence to quality, she selected a pair of ear-studs, a slender necklace and a matching bracelet. A dress watch was added, its sapphire diamond-studded face classifying it as an item of jewellery rather than a conventional timepiece.

'Mr Alvarez instructed me to present you with this.' The jeweller withdrew a rectangular velvet case and released the catch with the slight flourish of one about to display a magnificent surprise.

Kayla looked at the sapphires...the beautiful drop pendant, matching ear-studs, bracelet...and felt her stomach plummet.

'Where did you get these?' Was that her voice? It sounded incredibly hushed.

'Mr Alvarez acquired them a few years ago at an estate auction, I believe.' He passed a reverent finger over the stones. 'They were recently handed into my care to ensure the settings are intact.'

They had once belonged to her mother. A birthday gift in the days when Benjamin had been on top of his game.

The jeweller appeared to sense her disquiet. 'You do not like them?'

'They're beautiful.' Indeed they were, and had numbered high among Blanche's most loved pieces of jewellery. The question was why they were in Duardo's possession.

She stood in silence as the jeweller carefully packaged everything, provided valuation certificates and handed the glossy bag into Spence's safekeeping.

It was almost five when she entered the house, and on determining Duardo's whereabouts she made for his home office.

He glanced up from examining graphs and figures on his laptop, saved the data then swivelled in his chair to face her, noting her air of determination, the deep brilliance in her eyes…and waited for the fall-out.

'A successful day?'

The mildness of his voice merely strengthened her resolve. 'I want to thank you.' She paused almost imperceptibly. 'The diamonds. The watch.' She sounded incredibly polite, even to her own ears. 'They're fitting gifts to showcase the wife of a billionaire.'

He leant back in his chair and regarded her steadily. 'You've developed an aversion to jewellery?'

The brilliance intensified. 'No.'

'Then I don't see the problem.'

'It doesn't concern you that I do?'

'Not in the least.'

She wanted to hit him. Instead she stood her ground and aimed for controlled politeness, despite her inwardly seething anger. 'You bought Blanche's sapphires.'

His eyes sharpened, then became slightly hooded. 'I bid for them successfully. Yes.'

'Why?'

He uncoiled his body with lithe ease and moved around to lean one hip against the desk. 'Is the *why* of it so important?'

'Yes, dammit!' She eyed a paperweight on his desk and mentally weighed throwing it at him.

'Don't.' The silky warning held a lethal quality.

A host of conflicting thoughts clouded her features, and he defined each and every one of them.

'You deserve to have something that belonged to your mother.'

She didn't believe him. Couldn't.

'Then.' She struggled with the knowledge. 'Even *then* you were planning our remarriage?'

His eyes hardened and became bleak. 'It was never in doubt.'

Her chin tilted. 'And Benjamin?' She couldn't help herself. 'Did you plot his downfall?'

'Your father managed that of his own accord.'

So much fine anger seething beneath the surface. He had a mind to take and tame it into something else.

With one easy movement he tunnelled his hand through her hair and cupped the back of her head, while the other hand slid down to her waist and drew her close.

She didn't have time to utter a word as his mouth closed

over hers, then angled in possession as he plundered at will, using his tongue, the edges of his teeth to subdue and seduce until he sensed her capitulation, caught the faint groan of despair deep in her throat…and coaxed her response.

It was a while before he lifted his head, and he viewed the deep, slumberous quality evident in her eyes, the slightly parted swollen mouth…and resisted the temptation to take it to another level.

Kayla almost swayed beneath his probing gaze, and she fought against the shimmering tension, aware one wrong move, a castigating word would unleash an emotion she didn't want to deal with.

Instead she stood her ground and aimed for controlled politeness. 'If you'll tell me how long before we need to leave.'

He checked his watch. 'An hour and a quarter.'

'I'll ensure I'm ready on time.'

It wasn't the best exit line, but it would do.

CHAPTER FIVE

'DUARDO, *darling.*'

Kayla watched as the society matron did the air-kiss thing and followed it with a coquettish chuckle.

'And this is your wife.' She turned towards Kayla. 'How lovely to meet you, my dear.' The smile was a little too bright. 'The newsprint photograph didn't do you justice.'

The restaurant, the photographer.

The media hadn't failed to produce caption, photograph and an interesting piece for the morning's newspapers.

Tonight was indisputably *showtime.*

Hence the gown, the jewellery.

She'd chosen taffeta in a rich midnight-blue, with a fitted bodice and slender full-length skirt. Matching stilettos added height, and the colour highlighted the creamy texture of her skin, accented the smooth lines of her blonde upswept hair. The newly purchased jewellery provided a perfect finishing touch.

'Thank you.'

'Duardo has kept you a well-guarded secret.'

Act. A stunning smile curved her lips. 'Yes, hasn't he?'

Duardo caught hold of her hand and lifted it to brush

his lips to her palm. 'With good reason.' His eyes held hers, darkly captivating and infinitely seductive.

Hell, he was good.

'We shall expect you both at the Leukaemia Foundation dinner.'

He released her hand and gave the society doyenne his attention. 'Of course.'

'Overkill,' Kayla commented quietly when the woman moved out of earshot.

'You think?' He sounded mildly amused, and she offered a sweet smile.

'Definitely.'

'Ah, but there are certain…expectations, wouldn't you agree?'

'We get to play pretend.'

'Will it be so difficult?'

'I shall give it my best,' she assured with mock solemnity.

He looked incredible in a black evening suit, white dress shirt and black bow tie. Fine tailoring…Armani or Zegna? Together with handcrafted Italian shoes, gold cufflinks, an elegant watch and a touch of very expensive cologne.

It wasn't his clothing which drew attention, but the man who wore it. There was something dark and untamed beneath the sophisticated surface…a wary primitiveness apparent in the depths of his eyes that had the potential to both frighten and fascinate.

Undoubtedly for some women, it was a powerful aphrodisiac.

As it had been for her, at first. Except she'd caught a glimpse of the child he had been, the boy hardened by street-life and the need to stay one step ahead of the law in order to survive.

'You certainly know how to spring a surprise.'

The male voice held a degree of mockery, and Kayla slowly turned to face its owner. Not someone she knew, and, if first impressions were any indication, not a man she'd trust.

'Congratulations are in order.'

He made it sound like a condemnation instead of a compliment.

'Max.' Duardo's acknowledgment held cool politeness.

An eyebrow arched in silent query. 'No introduction, Duardo?'

There was something apparent, barely hidden beneath the surface, which she couldn't quite pinpoint.

'My wife, Kayla.' He paused almost imperceptibly. 'Maximillian Stein. The actress Marlena's husband.'

Max bowed. 'Marlena is indisposed. She sends her regrets, and her congratulations on your very recent marriage.' His smile held pseudo-pleasantness. 'Née Enright-Smythe, and your ex. Interesting.'

His expressionless gaze speared hers as he extended a hand, which she took out of politeness, hating the deliberate way his fingers curled over her own before she could pull them free. 'A rescue mission, or revenge?'

Kayla spared Duardo an adoring look. 'Shall I tell him, darling? Or will you?'

She lifted a hand to his cheek, felt the smooth warmth of his skin and managed not to blink when he covered her hand with his own.

'By all means share, *querida*.'

She turned towards Max. 'Romance,' she revealed sweetly. 'True love.'

Max's gaze narrowed, and she kept her voice light, sweet. 'Perhaps you've yet to experience it.'

He executed a slightly mocking bow. 'I'm so pleased for you.'

'Thank you.' Her tone was the model of decorum, and she waited until he moved away before meeting Duardo's steady gaze.

'You don't like him.'

Duardo's expression remained unchanged. 'I have reason not to trust him.'

'He's an associate?'

'From the days of my youth in New York.'

'I see.'

His mouth formed a wry twist. 'I doubt you do.'

'You share a rivalry.'

It was more than that. Whereas he had cleaned up years ago and only dealt legitimately…Max ran with wolves of another creed beneath the carefully constructed cover of respectability.

If it hadn't been for Marlena's father, he'd have severed all ties long ago. Except he owed a debt, one he'd promised to honour. And he had. Fostering Marlena's career, helping making her the *name* she was today.

'Isn't this fun?'

Duardo cast Kayla a look that held musing humour, and she offered him a beauteous smile before letting her gaze skim over the room.

A strange prickling sensation hit the back of her neck, and she turned slightly to find herself the object of Max Stein's studied appraisal.

It was more than interest, and strangely indefinable. Worse, it made her feel uncomfortable…almost afraid.

Soon the ballroom doors would open with the request everyone be seated at their designated tables.

In the past she'd attended many such events, as her parents had been strong supporters of various charities.

Another lifetime, she mused wryly, when she'd taken her father's wealth and social standing for granted.

Now she had no such illusions about life…or love. And she was back on the social scene as Duardo's wife.

Would the knives be out, and, if so, who would hold them?

Duardo Alvarez was a powerful man. Few would dare risk crossing him. Yet there were those who might not have the same reservations about his wife, given the speculation surrounding her background circumstances.

'Congratulations, darlings.'

Kayla turned to see a stunning brunette whose features were vaguely familiar.

'Elyse,' Duardo greeted warmly.

Of course. Model, tall, impossibly slender, with curves in all the right places, and utterly gorgeous. Known as *the face* of a major cosmetics company.

Elyse sent Kayla a sparkling glance. 'I was beginning to despair of him.'

'Really?' What else could she say?

'Companion of many, but lover of few.'

There were times when words were superfluous, and she settled for a musing smile.

'Catch you later.' With a waft of exotic perfume Elyse faded into the crowd.

'Was that meant to be reassurance, do you think?' Kayla arched sweetly, and caught the slight humour evident in those dark eyes.

'The ballroom doors have just opened.' He placed a hand at the back of her waist. 'Shall we go in?'

The table they were directed to held prominent position,

and Kayla's stomach sank a little as she saw one of the city's social doyennes already seated there.

Marjorie Markham and her husband. Tom? Or was it Tim? Hostess *par excellence*, with a dangerous tongue, the woman was a purveyor of gossip and known to take fact and embellish it with fiction.

Oh, *joy.*

Benito and Samara Torres appeared, and following an affectionate greeting, Samara took a seat next to Duardo.

The remaining six seats were soon filled by a judge and his wife, one of the city's scions and his partner and a mother and daughter.

An eclectic mix guaranteed to evoke interesting conversation based on superficial politeness, Kayla perceived a trifle wryly, aware nuances and practised manipulation formed part of the social game people played.

Drinks waiters circled the tables, pouring complimentary wine and accepting orders, followed by the charity's chairperson, who took the podium to provide an introduction, a list of past achievements together with a projection of future aims before wishing the guests an enjoyable evening.

'I doubted you'd show tonight. No honeymoon, darling?' Samara arched as waiters began serving the entrée. 'If I recall correctly, you didn't manage one the first time round.' She lifted her goblet of wine and gestured a toast. 'To the bride and groom.'

Oh, my. This had all the makings of being a *fun* evening.

'Hawaii,' Marjorie Markham announced with the satisfaction of remembered knowledge. 'You originally married there.'

'Indeed.' Duardo's accented drawl was pure silk. A silent warning the subject was off-limits, and one only the foolhardy would ignore.

Fortunately the waiters provided a diversion, and the focus shifted to food.

Kayla was supremely conscious of Duardo's close proximity, the occasional touch of his hand, his warm smile—purely for appearance's sake—and her own in reciprocation.

Playing the game, she perceived a trifle wryly.

Yet there was awareness beneath the surface, a heightened sense of the sensual magic he seemed to exude with effortless ease. Each time she looked at him, she had no difficulty imagining how his mouth felt on her own...as it trailed her body to tease sensitive pleasure pulses.

Oh, for heaven's sake! It's just sex...albeit mind-blowing, but just *sex* none the less.

So...*enjoy*, why don't you? To imagine there might be more was crazy. To *want* more...let's not go there! She dared not, for fear it might be more truth than she could bear.

At that moment Duardo turned towards her, his dark eyes inscrutable for several time-spinning seconds, then his mouth curved into a faint smile...almost as if he'd read her mind.

To compound it, he brushed his fingers down her cheek. And watched her melt a little.

It's only an act, she assured, and did some acting of her own by sending him a sparkling *sensual* smile, silently challenging him with a deliberate *two can play this game* look.

'Really, darling, get a room, why don't you?' Samara suggested, and her pouting moue reflected a degree of mocking humour which didn't reach her eyes.

'The preliminary teasing is part of the fun, don't you agree?' Kayla responded without missing a beat.

It was doubtful anyone other than Duardo could hear their conversation against the background noise, although retreat was probably a wise option.

Entertainment was provided between courses, and first up was the obligatory fashion parade, with waif-thin models displaying the latest in overseas designer wear bearing exorbitant price tags, and vied for by the social set's fashionistas.

The mother and daughter team made notes on their programmes; so, too, did Samara.

'That particular gown is *mine*.'

Benito Torres offered an indulgent smile at his wife's determined proclamation, at the exquisite sapphire silk chiffon with its multi-layered skirt, while the mother and daughter shot Samara a glittering *in your dreams* look that was quickly masked.

Kayla tamped down a mental image of all three women making a concerted dash in a bid to be first to secure the designer original.

'A gown I've reserved as a gift for my wife.' Duardo's indolent drawl earned him the unsolicited attention of all four women.

'Really?' Samara was the first to recover as she turned towards Kayla. 'Congratulations. I would have killed for it.' And she shot Benito a telling glare, while the mother uttered, 'Unfair,' to her daughter.

'How generous, darling,' Kayla managed sweetly, inwardly hating the public spectacle that seemingly emphasized her position as Duardo's trophy wife.

'My pleasure.' His answering smile left no one in any doubt as to what form that pleasure would take.

Oh, my. What a way to make enemies. If looks from those three women could kill, she'd be dead.

A comedian took the podium between the main and dessert courses, and a popular vocalist performed two numbers while the waiters served coffee.

With the evening's planned events at a close, it left guests the option to catch up with friends seated elsewhere in the ballroom.

Kayla barely held back her relief when Duardo indicated they should leave, although their passage from the ballroom was interrupted at frequent intervals by several fellow guests offering their congratulations.

'Nothing to say?' he queried with faint mockery as the Aston Martin purred through the city streets.

She spared him a sober look. 'I'm all talked out.' Smiled out, too. And she had the beginnings of a headache.

The evening, her first among guests as Duardo's wife, was over. She'd held her own with a degree of dignity. Except it was only the first of many, and it would be a while before their marriage ceased being the current topic of thinly veiled speculation.

'Please tell me I'm not in line to beard the lion's den again any time soon.'

'That bad, huh?'

Not really. Just that she was out of practice. 'It's been a long hiatus between social appearances,' she informed dryly, and glimpsed his mouth curve in the dim interior of the car. She felt compelled to add, 'Women home in on you like bees seeking a honeypot.'

'That bothers you?'

Big-time. Except she had no intention of telling him so. 'Should it?'

He brought the car to a halt inside the garage and cut the engine.

'I couldn't fault you.'

'A compliment, Duardo?'

'You find it difficult to accept I might gift you one?'

She offered him a startlingly direct look. 'Yes.' She reached for the door clasp with one hand and released her seat belt with the other.

He let her go, mirroring her actions with his own as he accompanied her into the house and watched as she made straight for the staircase.

Duardo reset the security alarm, minimized the main interior lighting system and followed her at a leisurely pace.

'Problem?'

Kayla heard the smooth silkiness in his voice as she made a third attempt at releasing the safety catch on her necklace, and offered, 'Nothing I can't handle.'

For heaven's sake, the catch had been easy to close …why was it so difficult to release?

'Allow me.'

His fingers touched hers, and she reacted as if she'd been burnt by a flame. To stand quiescent almost robbed the breath from her throat.

Fool. She'd been in his company for the past several hours. Why now was it any different?

Because they were alone in the bedroom. He was standing far too close for comfort. And she had no illusions as to how the night would end.

Worse, she wanted what he could give her. The stirring of her emotions…dammit, the *passion*. To lose herself in the sensual nirvana only he could provide.

To believe, if only for a while, that what they shared was real…as it had once been.

Except you could never go back. There was only *now.*

Was it her imagination, or did his fingers linger at her nape as he freed the catch?

She heard the faint chink as he placed the necklace down onto the bedside pedestal, then he caught hold of her shoulders and turned her round to face him.

He'd discarded his jacket, removed his bow tie and freed the top few buttons of his shirt.

Kayla met the darkness in his eyes with fearless regard, and barely quelled the faint hitch in her breath as he reached for the zip fastening on her gown.

'I can undress myself.' Her voice sounded stiff, and she glimpsed the way the corners of his mouth curved in humour.

'And deprive me of the pleasure?'

'As long as you don't expect me to reciprocate.'

The zip slid free, and she didn't move as it slithered down onto the carpet in a heap of silk.

All that separated her from total nudity was a slender thong brief, and her hands automatically lifted to shield her breasts in a gesture of modesty.

Unnecessary, given he knew their weight, texture, the sensitive peaks, how they tasted…and her reaction to his touch.

He lifted a hand and traced the curve of her waist, felt the slight quiver of her flesh beneath his touch and felt momentary satisfaction. 'Why so shy?'

Faint colour tinged her cheeks and her eyes deepened and became stormy. 'Don't *play* me.'

'Is that what you think I'm doing?'

'Aren't you?' she demanded, sorely tried, as his fingers brushed her navel, then slid slowly down to trace the seam of her thong.

The silent scream for him to desist remained locked in her throat as his finger hooked beneath the narrow seam and slid it down with practised ease.

His eyes held hers as he released the remaining buttons on his shirt, then pulled it free and tossed it over the valet frame. In seeming slow motion he toed off his shoes, his socks then he undid and removed his trousers.

'I don't want to do this.' The words left her lips in a shaky undertone.

Liar. Every nerve-end in her body was alive and vibrating with need. Worse, sensation spiralled deep within, making a mockery of the emotions she strove so hard to suppress.

His arousal was a potent force beneath the black silk barely sheathing its powerful rigidity, and she felt her insides clench in anticipation of his possession.

'No?'

He sounded almost amused, damn him, and her eyes flashed blue fire as he cupped her face, then fastened his mouth over her own.

His tongue traced the firm line of her lips, angling a little as she held back in a senseless stubborn gesture that had him nibbling the soft lower lip with the edges of his teeth, followed seconds later by a painful nip.

Her mouth parted in silent protest and his tongue swept hers, teasing in an evocative dance that was all persuasive mastery.

She didn't stand a chance.

Although the knowledge didn't stop her initial resistance, and she balled her hands into fists as she aimed for his shoulders, his back, anywhere she could connect with.

Only to give in with a stifled groan of despair as he cupped her bottom and lifted her against him, parting her thighs so the highly sensitized clitoris nestled against his erection.

Dear heaven.

Sensation arrowed deep within, radiating with pulsing intensity as he slowly slid her against him, creating an unbelievable friction that swept her to the brink…and he held her as she shattered.

'You don't play fair.' Her voice was little more than a husky whisper as his lips nuzzled the sensitive curve of her neck.

'Did you expect me to?'

He adjusted her slightly as he discarded his briefs, and she cried out at the skin-on-skin contact, the deep, pulsing need as he positioned her to accept his length…the long slow slide as she sank down on him.

The slick heat, the slight stretch of silken tissues as he reached the hilt…and began to move, slowly at first, until she caught his rhythm and their desire became rawly primitive, wild.

Almost beyond reason as he carried her to the bed and assaulted her senses until she lost all reason, every concept of where or who she was…except *his*.

His woman.

Only his.

CHAPTER SIX

THERE had to be a reason for each day, Kayla reflected as she folded the morning's newspaper and finished her coffee.

It didn't seem so long ago she'd wished for time to spare, not to have to rush from one job to the next, eating on the run, with one day seemingly merging into another.

Conferring with Maria was a token exercise, for the housekeeper and her husband maintained a well-established routine that needed no guidance or interference.

Retail therapy for the sake of it didn't hold much appeal. Besides, recent shopping expeditions had done much to provide her with clothes, shoes and lingerie for every occasion.

Establishing a social diary was something she'd prefer to forestall as long as possible. Invitations were beginning to appear to one social luncheon or another under various guises...some genuine, others merely a reason for the wives of wealthy city men to play dress-up and congregate together.

She'd been there, done that...taking time off at her father's instigation to ensure her face, her name made the social pages as the daughter of Benjamin Enright-Smythe.

Fêted…until life had taken a downward turn, so-called friends became elusive and invitations ceased.

Now the thought of filling her days with regular visits to the manicurist, hairdresser, beauty therapist in search of self-beautification held little appeal

The insistent burr of her cellphone interrupted her thoughts, and she picked up.

'Spence. Enquiring if you need my services this morning?'

Kayla made a split-second decision. 'Would you mind dropping me into the city?' She checked her watch. 'In about forty minutes?'

'I'll have the car waiting out front.'

It didn't take long to change into a smart business suit. Black, straight skirt, beautifully cut jacket. Tights, stilettos, minimum jewellery, skilfully applied make-up, her hair swept into a smooth knot.

Her CV bore her maiden name…Smythe, minus the hyphened Enright.

Personal presentation mattered in her bid to canvass a few employment agencies, and she bade Spence a bright 'Thanks' as she slid out from the car onto the busy city street. 'I'll get a taxi home.'

He shook his head. 'We've already done this. Duardo's instructions. Phone when you're ready and I'll swing by to collect you.'

The concept of having Spence at her beck and call seemed ridiculous. She could drive, she had a licence…she really needed a car of her own!

'This afternoon?' Kayla hazarded. 'After I've visited Jacob in hospital.'

'You haven't forgotten the foreign-film festival begins this evening?'

She closed her eyes, then opened them again as she recalled the agenda.

A premiere, filmed in Madrid with Spanish actors, subtitled in English, and attended by members of the Spanish Consulate, various dignitaries and society mavens.

'Got it. Cinema at seven, cocktails, socialize, seated at seven forty-five for an eight o'clock start.'

Note to self…purchase diary, check the week's upcoming social events and write them down.

Kayla did a swift mental calculation. Hawking her CV, lunch, hospital… 'Four o'clock outside the main hospital entrance? If there's any change, I'll phone you.'

'Take care.'

Was it her imagination, or did his words hold a hidden meaning?

Oh, for heaven's sake, get a grip, she silently castigated as the Lexus pulled out into traffic and moved swiftly from her line of vision.

The first agency went through the motions and politely insisted Kayla make an early-afternoon interview appointment. The second agency requested she return in an hour.

Time to sip a latte, call Jacob and browse through one of the city's major department stores.

Lunch was something light at a boutique café, and she entered Jacob's hospital room with a sense of satisfaction that both interviews had gone well; one particularly had sounded very positive, with a follow-up call promised the next day.

'Hi,' Kayla greeted with affection. 'You're looking great.'

'The orthopaedist is pleased, physiotherapist ditto.' He indicated the suite with a sweeping gesture. 'Great room, service, friendly nurses, pain management…' He offered her a teasing grin. 'The opportunity to flirt a little…What's not to like?'

'I've brought you a few things.' Books, the latest sports magazine, some personal clothing.

'Are you OK?'

Oh, heavens. 'What makes you think I might not be?'

His expression sobered, and his eyes held affectionate concern. 'Duardo. You. Marriage.'

He was too perceptive by far. 'It all worked out.' She summoned a smile and kept it in place.

'I'd like to think it has. For you.' He caught hold of her hand and threaded his fingers through her own. 'Thanks.'

Keep it light. There was no way she'd let him guess she was caught in a trap…an empty marriage, with no indication of how long it might last.

'For saving some of your skin?' She indicated his leg, the slowly fading bruises. 'You haven't exactly had an easy ride.'

'Nor you.'

'Hey,' she managed gently. 'We're a team.'

'Bro and sis for ever, huh?'

'Got it in one.'

They talked until visiting hours concluded, and a casual glance at the time had her reaching for her cellphone.

A few minutes later she cut the connection and stood to her feet.

'Spence is on his way.' She leant forward and brushed her lips to his cheek. 'Don't go climbing any cliffs.'

'As if.'

It was almost five when she entered the house, and she raced upstairs to shower, wash and dry her hair. Only to come to a halt at the sight of a large, glossy box resting on the bed.

The sapphire silk chiffon gown from the charity event,

neatly folded beneath layers of tissue paper. So he hadn't been joking. It was exquisite, and the exact shade of her mother's sapphires.

The comparison didn't escape her as she hung it carefully in her walk-in wardrobe. Had this been the reason behind Duardo's choice?

When she emerged into the bedroom Duardo was in the process of loosening his tie with one hand while freeing shirt buttons with the other.

The sight of him did strange things to her equilibrium. Olive skin, superb musculature…he emanated power from every pore of his body.

'Hi.' Good manners rose to the surface. 'The gown was delivered while I was out. It's beautiful. Thank you.'

He inclined his head, and his dark eyes swept her features and lingered a little. 'How was your day?'

Was she being super-sensitive in imagining his query was not as innocuous as it seemed?

'Fine.' Did Spence report her every move? Kayla pulled on casual clothes. 'I spent time in the city, had lunch, then visited Jacob.' It was the truth, with a few omissions.

Duardo released the belt at his waist and undid his trousers. 'Maria is serving dinner in fifteen minutes.'

Time to select what she intended to wear, pop a few essentials into an evening purse then do something with her hair.

The form-fitting red silk, she determined, with its scooped neckline, spaghetti straps and fitted evening jacket in matching red silk. Stilettos, minimum jewellery.

Maria had prepared a seafood paella, and Kayla merely picked at it, settled for salad and declined wine in favour of iced water.

'Not hungry?'

She replaced her cutlery, and met his dark gaze with equanimity. 'Is that a problem?'

'Should it be?'

'If you'll excuse me, I'll go change and do the make-up thing.'

'I'll be up in five minutes.'

All he had to do was add a tie and shrug into his suit jacket, whereas she required ten minutes minimum.

She was almost done when he entered the bedroom, and she checked her mirrored image, added lip-gloss, another sweep with the mascara wand then she crossed to the bed, collected her evening purse and turned to face him.

The butterflies in her stomach executed a dangerous flip, and she forced them to settle.

Three years on, and she was as susceptible to him as she had been from very first sight.

There was something about him, some intrinsic magic she'd yet to define that stirred her senses and sent them spiralling out of control.

He had the power to possess her...mind, body and soul, and she continually fought a losing battle to retain a semblance of sensual sanity.

It was crazy. *Love* wasn't part of the equation. Yet she was drawn to him like a helpless moth to a flame.

Would she survive...or burn and die?

Survive, a silent voice attested. It was the only answer.

'Shall we leave?' Her voice was cool, her smile practised, and she glimpsed something shift in those dark eyes as he crossed to her side.

The theatre foyer was crowded when they entered it, and Kayla felt the customary warmth as Duardo laid his arm along the back of her waist.

An Important Message from the Editors

Dear Reader,

If you'd enjoy reading romance novels with larger print that's easier on your eyes, let us send you TWO FREE HARLEQUIN PRESENTS® NOVELS in our LARGER PRINT EDITION. These books are complete and unabridged, but the type is set about 20% bigger to make it easier to read. Look inside for an actual-size sample.

By the way, you'll also get a surprise gift with your two free books!

Pam Powers

Peel off Seal and Place Inside...

she'd thought she was fine. It took Daniel's words and Brooke's question to make her realize she was far from a full recovery.

She'd made a start with her sister's help and she intended to go forward now. Sarah felt as if she'd been living in a darkened room and someone had suddenly opened a door, letting in the fresh air and sunshine. She could feel its warmth slowly seeping into the coldest part of her. The feeling was liberating. She realized it was only a small step and she had a long way to go, but she was ready to face life again with Serena and her family behind her.

All too soon, they were saying goodbye and Sarah experienced a moment of sadness for all the years she and Serena had missed. But they ad each other now, and that's what

She held

Printed in the U.S.A.
Publisher acknowledges the copyright holder of the excerpt from this individual work as follows:
THE RIGHT WOMAN Copyright © 2004 by Linda Warren. All rights reserved.
® and ™ are trademarks owned and used by the trademark owner and/or its licensee.

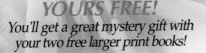

GET TWO FREE LARGER PRINT BOOKS!

YES! Please send me two free Harlequin Presents® novels in the larger print edition, and my free mystery gift, too. I understand that I am under no obligation to purchase anything, as explained on the back of this insert.

PLACE FREE GIFTS SEAL HERE

106 HDL EFU6   **306 HDL EFVJ**

FIRST NAME	LAST NAME

ADDRESS

APT.#	CITY

STATE/PROV.   ZIP/POSTAL CODE

Are you a current Harlequin Presents® subscriber and want to receive the larger print edition?

Call 1-800-221-5011 today!

▶ **DETACH AND MAIL CARD TODAY!** ▶

(H-PLPP-09/06) © 2004 Harlequin Enterprises Ltd.

The Harlequin Reader Service™ — Here's How It Works:

Accepting your 2 free Harlequin Presents® larger print books and gift places you under no obligation to buy anything. You may keep the books and gift and return the shipping statement marked "cancel." If you do not cancel, about a month later we'll send you 6 additional Harlequin Presents larger print books and bill you just $4.05 each in the U.S., or $4.72 each in Canada, plus 25¢ shipping & handling per book and applicable taxes if any.* That's the complete price and — compared to cover prices of $4.75 each in the U.S. and $5.50 each in Canada — it's quite a bargain! You may cancel at any time, but if you choose to continue, every month we'll send you 6 more books, which you may either purchase at the discount price or return to us and cancel your subscription.

*Terms and prices subject to change without notice. Sales tax applicable in N.Y. Canadian residents will be charged applicable provincial taxes and GST.

Proprietorial possession, protection…or *display*?

She told herself she didn't care as she slipped into an adopted part, lifting her face towards his and projecting a stunning smile.

'This promises to be a stimulating evening, darling.'

His mouth curved a little. 'Indeed.'

'Challenging,' she continued quietly, 'considering my knowledge of the Spanish language is severely limited.'

His fingers moved against the edge of her waist. 'I'm sure you recall a few important words.'

His voice was infinitely sensual, and a familiar, shivery sensation shook her slender frame.

Damn him. He was playing a deliberate game, evoking emotions…memories she tried so hard to suppress.

'Spoken with practised ease in the heat of the moment?'

He wanted to shake her…and almost did. 'Careful,' he warned quietly. 'At the end of the evening I get to take you home.'

She was playing with fire, and knew it. Yet her smile deepened. 'Is that a threat or a promise?'

'Your choice.'

'Duardo. Kayla,' a bright feminine voice intruded. 'How wonderful to see you.'

The both turned slightly to face one of the city's most prominent society matrons. Although *matron* was a misnomer, for Ashley Baines-Simmons was in her thirties and the wife of a man some twenty years her senior. A rare love match that had nothing to do with chronological age. Five years ago their marriage had caused a stir among the social set, with the usual slurs cast in aspersion. Yet Ashley had held her head high and sailed through it all with her integrity intact.

Sadly there was one very important difference.

Ashley had the unconditional love and support of her husband.

Kayla, on the other hand, suffered no illusions regarding Duardo's motivation.

'I can't begin to tell you how delighted I am to see you two back together again.'

Ashley brushed her lips to Kayla's cheek, then copied the action to Duardo.

'Our delight mirrors your own.' Duardo's response held practised warmth, and Kayla silently applauded his acting ability.

'We must get together,' Ashley declared. 'I'll be in touch.'

A waiter bearing a tray of canapés wove his way in their direction, followed by a waitress with a tray filled with flutes of champagne.

Kayla selected champagne, and took an appreciative sip, enjoying the slightly sharp taste, the faint bubbles.

'Duardo.'

Another sycophant? She turned slightly and instantly revised such a thought.

This woman was beautiful. Different. Dear heaven…breathtaking.

Actress? Model? *Former lover*?

'Jennifer,' Duardo acknowledged warmly and leaned forward to brush his mouth to her cheek.

Lover…definitely. Hopefully *former*. But not, Kayla perceived, too far distant, given the blatant message briefly evident and quickly hidden in the woman's liquid dark eyes.

OK, so you didn't expect him to remain celibate for three years, surely? Divorce gave him every moral right to bed any woman he chose.

It was *she* who hadn't been able to bear the thought of intimacy with anyone else.

'My wife, Kayla.'

The sound of Duardo's voice brought her sharply into the present, and with it…indecision.

Should she offer a smile? Handshake? Resort to the air-kiss thing? *Hell*, what was the protocol for the husband's wife and his ex-lover?

Jennifer made the first move by extending her hand. 'I'm so pleased to meet you.'

You are? Compliment, or contradiction?

Kayla took the woman's hand and played polite with a degree of genuine sympathy for any woman who'd loved and lost the man whose name she bore.

Duardo Alvarez was something else. Assuredly almost without equal. In bed and out of it.

Hadn't she hungered for his touch, wept for the loss of it? And now, experienced an emotional maelstrom as a result of the return of it?

Life, she determined a trifle grimly, held a certain irony.

'Enjoy the evening,' she evinced quietly.

'Thank you. I hope we'll have the opportunity to spend time with each other.'

Oh, my. With a view to what? Sharing coffee and confidences? Discussing Duardo?

Somehow she doubted the ex-lover and the current wife could ever be friends.

Jennifer melted into the crowd, and Kayla sent Duardo a mocking look in silent askance.

'Her husband was killed last year piloting a small plane in hazardous conditions during a snowstorm.'

'How noble of you to console the grieving widow.'

His eyes darkened. 'He was a friend. It was the least I could do.'

Where was her compassion? 'I'm sorry.'

One eyebrow lifted. 'For mistaking friendship for something else?'

There had been something else…on Jennifer's part, if not his. She was willing to swear to it. No woman looked at a man quite like that without being emotionally involved…even if it didn't lead to intimacy.

It was a relief when Duardo's attention was taken by one of the Spanish Embassy's dignitaries, and a personal introduction to the Spanish Ambassador.

Formality and politeness ruled, together with a degree of awe. Afterwards Kayla could barely recall a thing she'd said.

'You'd already met,' she managed quietly minutes later.

'Yes.' Duardo's acknowledgment held faint amusement. 'In New York.'

'Should I find that interesting?'

'Perhaps.'

'Although you've no intention of disclosing just *how* interesting.'

'No.'

It was a relief when the electronic buzzer sounded, summoning everyone to enter the theatre auditorium.

Relief that was short-lived when Samara Torres encouraged Benito towards the two vacant seats at Duardo's side.

Kayla leaned in close as the lights began to dim. 'Three conquests in one evening, *darling*? Perhaps you should give me a list.'

He took possession of her hand and threaded his fingers through her own. She dug the tips of her nails into his palm, and felt his grasp tighten in silent warning.

She bore his name, wore his ring and lived in his beautiful home.

Once she'd had his heart…something she doubted he'd gift her again.

The music began, the curtains parted electronically and the screen filled with Technicolor images.

Pathos, humour and temperament. Lost love, angst and misunderstanding, closing with found love and resolution.

The film had won plaudits at the Cannes Film Festival, the director was lauded for his interpretation and Kayla enjoyed the concept despite the captions in English making for slightly disjointed viewing.

Coffee was served in the foyer, and a number of the guests lingered, while others took their leave.

'Would you care to join Benito and I for coffee?' Samara named an upmarket coffee boutique in Double Bay.

'Thank you,' Duardo responded. 'Perhaps another time? I have an early-morning flight.'

Samara offered a disappointed pout that held overtones of petulance, and Kayla likened her image to a playful kitten…with claws.

'Say "goodnight", *querida*,' Benito instructed with thinly veiled mockery. 'We'll browse the café scene and find someone to amuse you.'

Were they for real, or simply game-playing?

'Benito likes to indulge her,' Duardo drawled as they walked to where their car was parked.

'How…generous of him.'

'She fulfils his needs.'

Now that was a comment open to interpretation, if ever there was one! 'Too much information,' she managed with an edge of mockery.

They reached the Aston Martin and he released the security mechanism, saw her seated then crossed round to slip in behind the wheel.

Soft, misty drizzle clouded the windscreen as he drew into the flow of traffic, and she watched the silent swish of wipers, the strong beams of light from oncoming cars.

Idle conversation for the sake of it escaped her, and she leaned back against the head-rest and closed her eyes.

He'd mentioned an early-morning flight. Where was he going, and how long would he be away?

Did it matter?

She told herself she didn't care…and knew she was kidding herself.

It was after eleven when they entered the house, and Kayla reached the main bedroom bare minutes ahead of him. Somehow she'd expected he'd check emails, stock options, graphs…whatever, before coming to bed.

She slipped off her shoes, removed jewellery, dispensed with her evening suit then crossed to the *en suite* to undress and deal with her make-up.

When she was done, she donned a towelling robe and emerged into the bedroom to discover Duardo in the process of discarding his shirt.

'Don't you have something you should tell me?'

Her eyes flew wide as he crossed to stand in front of her. Not good, for his close proximity had an effect on the tenure of her breathing.

'I can't think of a thing.'

He caught hold of her chin between thumb and forefinger, and tilted it so she had to look at him.

'Let me refresh your memory.' His drawled voice was pure silk. 'You had interviews with two city employment agencies today.'

Consternation jolted through her body, and she barely controlled her expression. 'You know this *because*…?'

'Our recent remarriage gained local and national news,' he reminded her wryly. 'How long did you imagine you'd remain incognito as Kayla *Smythe*?'

'Long enough to get a job on my own merit.'

Duardo shot her a measured look. 'You have no need to seek employment.'

'Don't you get it?' Her eyes assumed a fiery sparkle. 'I *want* to work.' She took a deep breath. 'To do something constructive with each day. Dammit, I'm not asking for your approval.'

'Good. Because you don't have it.'

She curled her hands into fists, and barely refrained from hitting him.

'Are you implying you'll blacklist me with every employment agency in town?'

He had the power to do it…and could, all too easily. 'Don't put words in my mouth.'

'You should have married a yes-woman who'd revel in the role of social butterfly,' she fired with unaccustomed vehemence.

'Instead, I have a pocket spitfire.'

His voice held silky amusement, and she lashed out at him. Only to find her wrist caught in a painful grip.

'You want to fight?'

She couldn't hope to win. He had the strength to outmatch her, and would, easily, without compunction. 'Yes, damn you!'

His expression remained unchanged, with the exception of his eyes. Dark, still and faintly hooded, they held something in their depths that sent chills scudding down the length of her spine.

She had no idea how long she stood there. Seconds…minutes. It was as if time stood still, the tension between them electric, volatile, where a word, a sudden move could unleash the unknown.

There was so much *more* at stake than the issue at hand. She hated that she owed him. Resented the balance of power was so heavily weighted against her.

Most of all, she hated herself for the compelling need he aroused in her…for him, only *him*.

It wasn't fair. None of it was fair.

Duardo watched the fleeting emotions chase her expressive features, and defined each and every one of them.

He could reach out and pull her in against him…make her his in a way that would dispel all thought, except the primitive joy of very good sex.

And he would…soon.

'It is so important you work?'

Kayla waited a beat. 'Yes.'

No reason, no qualification. 'You want to do this on your own?'

'I need to,' she managed simply.

It was impossible to determine anything from his silent scrutiny.

'If I were to offer you a position with one of my companies—'

Kayla didn't wait for him to finish. 'I'd refuse.'

'You intend arguing with me?'

'It's inevitable.' Kayla effected a light shrug and met his narrowed gaze. 'We have opposing viewpoints.'

One eyebrow slanted. 'Indeed.'

It would be all too easy to accept Duardo's offer. Stipulate flexi-hours, employment without pressure…

She struggled with her conscience, and won.

'I had the token employment in a prime office for a large salary with my father…and lived with the accusation of nepotism, the snide, behind-my-back innuendos from his associates and fellow staff.'

He recognized the challenge, the need to succeed, and silently applauded it…and her. For no other woman of his acquaintance would choose to take the more difficult path, given similar circumstances.

'What about setting up a business of your own?'

Kayla searched his expression for a degree of cynicism, and found none. 'You can't be serious?' She hardly dared breathe.

Something to put her heart and soul into creating, then completing with her own individual flair.

A pie-in-the-sky idea that had teased her mind for some time. Only to be discarded as not only unrealistic, but also impossible due to lack of funds and massive debts.

Now she had no problem recalling her vision of an upmarket bathroom-accessory boutique, with the finest towels…face, hand and bath towels, embroidered, lace borders, the finest Egyptian cottons. Luxurious soaps, bath oils, candles. Elegant cut-crystal bottles and jars, of the finest quality. Catering to the wealthy and lovers of beautiful wares.

Duardo felt something tug his gut as he watched her expressive features. Had she any idea how easy he found it to read her? The luminous quality apparent in her eyes, the softly parted mouth?

'Run it by me.'

He wouldn't go for it. Besides, she couldn't finance such a venture.

A tiny hysterical bubble of laughter rose and died in her throat. What was she *thinking?*

She gave a negligible shrug. 'I doubt it'll fly.'

He stroked his thumb over the fullness of her lower lip, and felt it tremble. 'Why not?'

Kayla just looked at him. 'Money.'

'I'm not averse to becoming a silent partner in a viable business proposition.'

She dared not get her hopes up. Yet it was impossible to still the excitement fizzing through her veins.

Oh, hell, what did she have to lose?

The words spilled out, tentatively at first, as she described the format, style, preferred location.

'Set everything on paper, get quotes, find suppliers and present me with a proposal.'

Just like that? She was almost speechless. 'You're kidding, right?'

'You'll need an office. I'll have Spence refurbish a room downstairs with the necessary equipment.'

She needed the venture to be hers. Something she strove and worked for. 'There's just one thing.' Her eyes speared his. 'If this works out, I insist everything you invest is in the form of a legitimate loan for which I'm responsible.'

'I'll see to it.'

'Thank you.'

'Are we done?'

'For now.'

'Good.' He lowered his head and covered her mouth with his own. One hand slid to cup her buttocks as he drew her close, and she leaned in, savouring his touch.

Here, like this, she could lose herself in him and pretend for a while that what they shared was *real*. More than just very good sex...the sensual magic of two people completely in tune with each other on every level.

As it had been when they'd made love for the first time. Before displaced family loyalty had intervened and her life began its downward spiral into an ever-deepening pit.

From which she'd been rescued...at a price.

The question was not whether the price was too high, but if she could survive with her pride and integrity intact.

The moment held a certain bitter sweetness.

Later, as she lay sated in his arms and dreamy in the post-coital aftermath, she told herself she didn't care.

There was time in the cool light of day for reality to surface, and the doubts and resentment to creep in.

But for now, on the edge of sleep, nothing else seemed to matter.

CHAPTER SEVEN

KAYLA woke to find she was alone in the large bed, and she hastily checked the time, groaned then hit the shower.

Duardo would be at the airport about to board his flight to Melbourne, where he'd be in meetings all day, and therefore incommunicado, emergencies notwithstanding.

Requesting his approved list of contractors didn't fall into the emergency category, she decided as she pulled on jeans, added a cotton top then twisted her hair into a careless knot atop her head.

Breakfast comprised fresh fruit, yoghurt, toast and coffee eaten on the terrace, and she had just poured her second coffee when Spence joined her, carrying a folder.

'Duardo suggested you might like to check through these.'

These were a comprehensive sheaf of papers detailing various contractors, shop-fitters, tradesmen. Another outlining real estate owned by the Alvarez consortium, together with properties up for tender in a few of the city's upmarket suburbs.

Kayla indicated a chair. 'Join me in a coffee.'

She skimmed through the paperwork with a sense of mounting disbelief. 'We only discussed this idea last night.'

'It was just a matter of accessing the computer and downloading the appropriate file.' He spooned sugar into his cup, then took an appreciative sip of coffee. 'This morning we'll check out locations, then we'll discuss your plans with an architect and designer to obtain an overview of what you require.'

'Today?'

'You sound surprised.'

She offered a rueful smile. 'I didn't expect such fast action.'

'Duardo has a certain reputation for getting things done.'

Without doubt. 'When do we hit the road?'

'As soon as you're ready.'

'Not the inner city,' Kayla specified as Spence swung the Lexus onto New South Head Road. 'Too much competition from the major stores.'

'Agreed. There are two possible locations, one in Double Bay that Duardo has recently added to his investment portfolio.'

If she could name the ideal location, Double Bay would top the list. She almost held her breath in the silent hope the property might be one of several old cottages converted and refurbished into boutiques. Tucked close side-by-side, they lined both sides of a street frequented by the city's social set in the heart of one of the city's most prestigious upmarket suburbs.

'You're kidding me,' she said with undisguised delight as Spence turned into the street and indicated one of the cottages.

'It's exactly *right* in every way.' She hardly realised she was voicing her thoughts. 'I had imagined a shop, one room. But this…' She spread her hands, lost for words.

The cottages were built very close together on pocket-handkerchief-sized land, each cottage small with no hallway, just each room opening onto the room immediately behind it.

'The lease has run out, the cottage forms part of a deceased estate and the family decided to sell.'

For a phenomenal figure. Had to be, given the location.

Spence found a parking space. 'Let's go look, shall we?'

Wooden floors, rich Oriental rugs, select apparel tastefully displayed. Spence presented the *vendeuse* with a card.

'Yes, of course. I've been notified to expect you.'

Two rooms, which could easily be opened up into one large room, if need be. With the requisite kitchen-utility room at the rear, followed by an antique bathroom.

It was perfect. Kayla tamped down her enthusiasm and summoned a degree of caution.

This was a major venture, involving major money.

Duardo's money.

What if her vision didn't succeed? What if a bathroom-accessory boutique in this area simply didn't fit the market?

Running a business wasn't for the faint-hearted. Clientele could prove remarkably fickle.

Spence spared her a discerning look as they reached the pavement. 'You have doubts?'

How could she explain? Or confide in him?

'It's an ideal position.'

'Prime.' He pulled out his cellphone. 'You want to check out the alternative location? Otherwise I'll contact the interior designer and tell him we're on our way.'

Nothing could beat this. 'Measurements, floor plan—'

'I have them. At this point you need to explain your ideas, what you envisage for the end result. He'll work from there, and send in sketches to scale for you to examine, amend and ultimately choose.'

She attempted to tone down her amazement. 'Just like that?'

'Just like that,' Spence reiterated with a flash of musing humour. 'He's worked with Duardo on a number of projects.'

It became a day like no other day, for the speed with which things were achieved and set in motion made her head spin.

'The existing tenant vacates the cottage at the end of the week,' Spence informed her as he headed the Lexus for home. 'If you decide any structural changes are required, the plans will be submitted to Council, and once they're approved the contractors will move in.'

Spence's cellphone rang and he picked up, listened, said, 'Yes, I'll tell her.' And cut the connection.

'Duardo. Unresolved issues. He'll stay overnight and continue negotiations tomorrow.'

The prospect of losing Duardo's disturbing presence for one night didn't faze her in the least. She wanted to double-check paperwork, set up her own sketches, determine the interior layout, stock agents.

At least she wasn't going into this blind. She *knew* what she wanted, how she needed the cottage to be set up.

There had been action at home, Kayla discovered at Josef's bidding, with a room next to Duardo's home office cleared and set up with a desk, cabinets, state-of-the-art laptop, printer, phone station.

Spence set the folder down on the desk. 'All yours,' he indicated smoothly. 'There's a wireless router, which allows you to access the internet from anywhere in the house.'

It was almost too much. 'Thank you. For everything you've done today,' she added.

He was, she knew, just following Duardo's instructions. They'd achieved far more than she had ever imagined possible in a day. Oh, go with honesty! She'd have been ecstatic if it had taken a week!

'You're welcome.'

He left, and Kayla wandered the room, touching the desk, the cabinets, then she examined the laptop, noted it was already set up with all the necessary software, and sank into a chair.

It was little wonder Duardo Alvarez had achieved billionaire status if this was an indication of his *modus operandi*.

Yet why was she so surprised?

Hadn't he moved on her with equal speed? Initially sweeping her off her feet to Hawaii and marriage?

What about *now*?

A hollow feeling encompassed her heart, her mind.

Had he stood by, deliberately waiting for the figurative axe to fall so she had no recourse but to turn to him?

Was remarriage a form of revenge?

She'd been convinced of it from the onset. So *sure*.

Yet—

The in-house phone rang, and she picked up.

'I can serve dinner in fifteen minutes, if it suits you.'

'That's fine, Maria. Thanks.'

Time to shower and change, then she'd seclude herself in the office and check out suppliers on the 'net.

It was almost seven when she re-entered the office, and she set to work with organised diligence. She knew the products she wanted: Excellent-quality milled soaps, exotic oils, beautiful packaging.

At some stage her cellphone rang, and she picked up, voiced an automatic 'hello', then heard Duardo's familiar drawl in response.

'You sound distracted.'

'Make that *overwhelmed*.'

His faint chuckle curled round her nerve-ends, and tugged a little.

'The day has gone according to plan?'

'Exceeded it, in spades.' She waited a beat. 'Thank you.'

'You can thank me when I get home.'

An erotic image came immediately to mind. One she was unsuccessfully able to dismiss. 'I think I can manage to do that.'

'Imagining *how* is liable to keep me awake and uncomfortable all night.'

'There's a remedy for it. Although I believe it's rumoured to send you blind.'

'Indeed?'

'I can't indulge in phone sex. I have work to do,' she managed primly, and heard his soft laughter.

'Now, there's an interesting concept.'

'Work?' It was fun to tease him from a distance.

'Goodnight, *querida*. Sleep well.' He cut the connection before she had a chance to respond.

It was late when she closed the laptop and ascended the stairs to bed.

Her mind was in overdrive, making it difficult to covet sleep, and when she did finally slip into somnolence she was consumed by dreams…harrowing episodes of the past, when she worked every waking hour and there was insufficient money to pay essential bills.

Kayla woke in the early hours, unaware in those brief

few seconds of where she was, the images so vivid in her head she could almost believe she was back in the tiny flat she'd shared with Jacob.

With shaky fingers she switched on the bedside lamp and experienced relief at the visual proof of *this* bedroom, Duardo's home…even if the large bed was lacking his presence.

Auto-suggestion, she reasoned as she dragged weary fingers through her hair.

New business. Money. Fear of failure.

She checked the time, saw it was almost dawn and knew she'd never settle back to sleep.

If Duardo were here, he'd reach for her…and channel her wakefulness into leisurely sex.

Thinking of their shared intimacy resulted in a languorous sigh, and she rolled over and thumped her pillow with a frustrated groan.

OK, so she'd dress, pad downstairs, make coffee, take it into her office…and work.

Breakfast was something she took a ten-minute break for, and she chose to eat lunch at her desk.

By late afternoon she'd refined a list of suppliers and narrowed it down to two. Luxury proved to be expensive, but the items were way above what could be found in department stores and speciality shops.

The designer had faxed through preliminary sketches, from which she took copies to play around with, pencilling in an old-fashioned bathtub on one side of the room and a hip-bath in the other. Towels, meticulously folded in stacks, featuring an artistic bath-sheet spilling from the top to enable the clientele to feel the superb texture without disturbing the stacks…in the same colour, multi-colours forming a glorious rainbow.

Shelving with cut-crystal jars in all shapes and sizes containing exotic bath salts, bath oils, scents.

She could see it, almost embrace the vision and delight in the subtle scents.

Scrubs, sponges, long-handled luxury brushes. Apothecary jars holding multi-coloured cotton balls...beautiful shower-caps. A skilful blend of old and modern.

Candles. Gorgeously scented in delicately coloured wax.

Kayla felt like a child as she took a box of pencils and shaded in the colours, watching the sketch come alive before her eyes.

Dinner became an intrusion, although she bowed to Maria's voiced wisdom in the need of food and offered praise for the dish the housekeeper had prepared.

Then she took her coffee back to the office and worked on the costings, profit margins. She needed to factor in lease payments, utilities, and consider the possibility of hiring part-time staff.

She'd also need her own transport. It was ridiculous to continue relying on Spence.

It was relatively easy to create graphs, projections, a tentative profit and loss account, tax expenditure...

It was there Duardo found her, fingers flying over the laptop keyboard, while stacks of paperwork sat neatly on the desk.

She was so totally absorbed she didn't realise he'd entered the room, and he stood observing the fierce look of concentration creasing her features, saw the tip of her tongue edge out, and noticed the way she caught her lower lip with her teeth.

Her hair looked as if she'd raked her fingers through it, and the once secure knot on top of her head looked in danger of total collapse.

Word had it she'd been sequestered in this room since dawn, with time out only for meals.

Enough, he decided, was enough, and at that moment she looked up, offered a startled smile and followed it with a huskily voiced, 'Hi, you're home.'

He crossed to her side, skimmed the screen and ran a light hand over her shoulders. 'Press the *save* button, and close it down for the night.'

'I'm almost done.'

'It'll keep.'

'Two minutes.'

'One,' he allowed, and watched her fingers fly.

Then she closed out of the programme, shut down the screen…and gave a sigh of pleasure as he began kneading the kinks from her shoulders, her neck.

Her eyelids fluttered down and she rolled her head, then simply enjoyed his ministrations.

It felt so good, and she commended him. 'Thank you.' He deserved more. She indicated the room. 'For all this,' she said simply. 'The Double Bay location is perfect.' His hands stilled and curved over her shoulders. 'Everything is happening so fast.' She broke off as he lifted her from the chair. 'What are you doing?'

'Taking you to bed.'

Kayla linked her hands at his nape as he moved from the room. 'I've worked longer hours than this,' she protested. Every day, for the past few years.

'I'm not doubting your stamina or strength of will.'

'Put me down,' she insisted as he ascended the stairs.

'Soon.'

He entered the bedroom, closed the door, slid her down then he cupped her face and kissed her…thoroughly.

She was too weary to think, or hesitate. Instead she

allowed her instincts to rule as she moved in close and kissed him back, exulting in his touch, the feel of him. His taste, the faint muskiness that was *his*...all male, a faint edge of cologne.

Dear heaven, this was good. So good.

She wanted more, much more, and her fingers sought the buttons on his shirt, freed them and savoured the feel of his skin, barely aware he'd unsnapped her jeans and was in the process of removing her top.

Her bra followed, and a helpless groan emerged from her throat as he cupped her breasts and began easing his thumbs back and forth over their burgeoning peaks.

Sensation spiralled through her body, heating it to fever-pitch, and she cried out as he buried his mouth against the sensitive curve at the edge of her neck.

His hands slid down and edged beneath her jeans to cup her bottom, and she reached for his belt, released it and freed the zip fastening of his trousers.

The size and force of his erection almost undid her, and she stroked it gently, heard his faint primitive growl and she gasped as he lifted her high to attach his mouth to one sensitive breast.

Kayla curved her legs over his hips and held on.

Their clothes became a hindrance, and were soon dispensed with, then his mouth possessed hers in a kiss that shattered her completely.

'Share my shower.'

It wasn't an invitation, but a statement of intent, and she didn't think...didn't *want* to think as he carried her into the large shower stall and set the water temperature gauge.

Skin soon became slick with soap and water as they took pleasure in cleansing each other, playful, daring and incredibly sensual until it wasn't enough.

In one easy movement Duardo lifted her high and she wrapped her legs around his waist, then sank onto him, loving the erotic sensation as she took all of him, then held on as they caught a rhythm...long, slow strokes that nearly drove her wild, until she took the initiative and sent him to the edge.

And exulted in the sense of power as he lost control.

It was a while before they turned off the water, caught up towels then, dry, slid between the sheets.

'My turn, hmm?' Duardo moved over her and trailed kisses down her throat, savoured the soft swell of her breasts and teased each tender peak with the edges of his teeth before moving to her waist, caressing her abdomen. Then he sought the aroused clitoris and bestowed the most intimate kiss of all...holding her hips as his tongue, the delicate nip of his teeth, became more than she could bear.

Let go, a silent voice encouraged, and she held back until she shattered, splintering into a thousand pieces, sobbing uncontrollably with an emotion so intense she lost all sense of who or where she was.

He held her close, his lips caressing her cheek as his hands soothed a pattern up and down her spine. He murmured words she didn't understand, and kissed her so gently she was unable to stem the slow trickle of tears.

Magic. Evocative. Libidinous. Myriad sensations defying adequate description.

Once, she'd called it *love*. Convinced her primitive hunger for this man and how he made her feel could only be that ultimately prized emotion.

Dear God, what an innocent she'd been.

CHAPTER EIGHT

A PRIVATE dinner party…her first as Duardo's wife, where impressions and image vied with the importance of the invitation.

Kayla selected classic black in a fitted design whose lines hugged her slender curves. The wide scooped neckline displayed her cream-textured skin, and she added the diamond pendant Duardo had gifted her, then fixed the matching ear-studs.

Hair was swept into a smooth twist and held in place with a glittery comb, while her make-up was understated with subtle emphasis on her eyes, the curve of her mouth.

The dress came with a matching fitted jacket, and she slipped it on, cast her mirrored image a brief overall glance then collected her evening purse and crossed to Duardo's side.

He looked magnificent, as always. Faultless tailoring, crisp cotton shirt, silk tie. A flash of gold at his wrist. Freshly shaven, gorgeous…and hers.

She bore his name, occupied his bed and in the dark night hours it was almost possible to believe there was no past…only the present, and a glimpse of what the future might hold.

The doubts, the insecurities, came with the daylight, when she unconsciously searched his expression, examined his mood, every word...and attempted to analyse each nuance for any hidden meaning. Only to silently castigate herself for wanting the impossible.

'Whenever you're ready to leave.'

His smile was swift and held an edge of mockery. 'And face the social jungle?'

'Ah, you're familiar with the terrain,' Kayla offered lightly and saw one eyebrow slant.

'And the cats?'

She rolled her eyes 'I gather we're not talking the domestic variety?'

Duardo placed a hand at the edge of her waist. 'Behave.'

'Always.'

The venue was a gracious stately home in suburban Vaucluse, high on the hill with panoramic views over the harbour.

Several luxury cars lined the driveway, and Kayla steeled herself for the evening ahead as Duardo brought the Aston Martin to a halt.

Their hosts were a charming couple...an associate of Duardo's and his wife. Plus ten guests, six of whom Kayla recognized from previous social occasions attended as Benjamin's daughter. An actress and her much older producer husband, Max, a noted author and his PA made up the other four, with introductions completed.

The beautiful people, Kayla silently accorded without rancour, each one of whom was groomed, trained from birth to play a certain part. The right schools, holidays abroad, command of at least one other language, the requisite gap year overseas.

She had been one of them, once. Until her circumstances changed and she discovered the hard way that so-called friends were notoriously fickle.

Now, as Duardo's wife, she was being welcomed back into the fold with open arms and voiced delight.

Genuine or superficial? She wasn't sure she wanted to do the maths.

How long would it take for someone to ask the predictable query about her remarriage?

Perhaps politeness would reign, and curiosity would remain unvoiced.

Did piglets fly?

Flutes of champagne and social conversation. She could do that. She'd had plenty of practice, and she summoned sufficient warm charm as she circulated at Duardo's side.

It was interesting to engage the writer in conversation, to laud his success in the marketplace and enquire about his work-in-progress.

'I have a valid reason not to discuss it.'

She inclined her head in silent acknowledgement. 'While it's between you and the computer screen, it remains sacrosanct?'

His eyes took on a musing gleam. 'You comprehend the creative process.'

Her smile was genuine. 'Perhaps refine that to believing discussing it too much could jinx the end result?'

'Ah, *touché*.' He arched an eyebrow. 'Might one assume you have a creative endeavour in mind?' He gave a soft chuckle and touched a telling finger to the side of his nose. 'Enough said.'

'What, darling, is *this* all about?' His PA copied his action as she moved to join them, and the look the woman cast him was tellingly intimate.

Intriguing, Kayla determined as a fellow guest engaged Duardo in conversation.

She began moving towards their hostess, only to be forestalled by the actress.

'Marlena,' Kayla acknowledged, and controlled the faint sinking feeling in her mid-section at the thinly disguised disregard evident.

'Duardo has tickets for my opening night.'

The stage? She'd have to brush up on what and who was currently in vogue, and a name. 'We'll look forward to your performance.'

'He's never missed an opening night since he left you.'

She longed to correct the actress that it was *she* who had walked away. Instead, she summoned a polite smile. 'Really?'

'Duardo is one of my most ardent fans.'

Marlena wanted her to believe it was more than that, Kayla deduced. Why?

Oh, for heaven's sake, she dismissed in self-denigration. As if you don't know!

'*Querida*,' a familiar voice drawled close by, and Kayla turned towards Duardo with a brilliant smile, ensuring it didn't falter as he threaded his fingers through her own and brought their joined hands to his lips.

It bore every evidence of loving devotion. Except, only she glimpsed the darkness in his eyes, the silent probing query she chose to dismiss.

He turned towards the woman at her side. 'Marlena.'

The actress's smile alone could have won her plaudits. 'Darling, I was just telling Kayla you're one of my most ardent fans.'

'Indeed?'

A suitably innocuous response, if ever there was one.

'You'll excuse us?' Duardo continued.

'Just when it was becoming interesting,' Kayla declared quietly as he led her towards two fellow guests.

'Marlena enjoys—' His pause provided the opportunity for her to intercept.

'You?'

'Creating drama, for the sake of it,' he concluded, and she inclined her head in all seriousness.

'Ah, living the soap opera, huh?'

'Remind me to take you to task when we're alone.'

She offered a stunning smile. 'Oh, *darling*, why wait?'

He didn't, and she cursed herself for issuing the challenge as his mouth closed over hers in an erotic kiss that brought soft colour to her cheeks and left her feeling vaguely mortified.

It took every effort to summon a misty smile and lay her palm against his cheek in a seemingly intimate gesture.

A gesture he compounded by moving his head slightly to press his lips to her palm.

It was all she could do not to utter 'you win'. Except that would have spoilt the display.

Now, there's the thing…if he was intent on making a silent statement, who was it aimed at? Marlena?

Dinner comprised an elaborate collection of small courses…ten in all. Each a superb compliment to the catering firm their hosts had hired for the evening.

Having served restaurant tables, Kayla could only wonder at the number of matching dinner sets used, the constant replacement of exquisite Cristofle flatware.

Entertaining was an art form, and one at which their hosts excelled. The planning alone would have taken days, involving consultations over the choice of dishes, wine, even the blend of coffee.

It had been something her mother had taken pride in during the days when Benjamin's business boomed and money was no object.

How things changed, Kayla reflected, glad her mother hadn't had to witness Benjamin's downfall. It would have killed her to be cast aside by the very people she considered to be her friends. To have to downgrade from her magnificent harbour-front home.

'We are always in need of valuable members of the community to give their time to help raise funds for the sick and the needy. Would you be interested in helping out, my dear?'

Kayla replaced her goblet of water, and gave their hostess her attention.

'I'll need to confer with Duardo. We've yet to define my daytime role.'

'Darling,' Marlena offered with pseudo-sweetness, 'no one could be in any doubt as to your night-time role.'

It was almost possible to hear the collective indrawn breath of their fellow guests.

Oh, my. Marlena wanted to fight dirty? In public?

'You would insult me?' Kayla responded quietly.

Marlena chose not to answer, and the author's PA sought to defuse the situation with a change of subject.

It wasn't over. Not by any stretch of the imagination. Unless she was mistaken, it was important for Marlena to score…and she hadn't.

Coffee was served in the lounge, and it was almost a relief when Duardo indicated they would leave.

'No recriminations?' she posed when he eased the car towards Point Piper.

'Why would you think I might offer any?'

'For a few minutes it wasn't pretty in there.'

He cast her a dark glance as he paused at a set of traffic lights. 'You gave as good as you got.'

Yes, she had. Except there was no satisfaction to it. And unless she was mistaken, she'd made an enemy. One who'd feel compelled to strike back.

Kayla chose silence during the long minutes it took to reach Point Piper, and indoors she made straight for the stairs, uncaring whether he followed or not.

'I'll be up soon.'

His voice held an element of something she didn't care to define. 'Don't rush. I need to prepare for my night-time role.' Stupid, foolish words that held an edge she hadn't intended as they spilled from her lips without thought.

'Kayla.' A single word, yet it held infinite warning.

She didn't pause or turn towards him, and seconds later she cried out in shocked surprise as strong hands gripped her waist and lifted her bodily over one masculine shoulder.

'Put me down!'

Duardo kept on walking, and she balled a hand into a fist and hit him *hard*...with no effect whatsoever.

'You fiend! What do you think you're doing?'

He reached their bedroom and closed the door so quietly, she could almost wish he'd slammed it. Then he released her down onto her feet.

She'd lost one stiletto, and she slid out of the other...bad move, for she lost valuable inches.

'Let's get one thing clear.' His voice was quiet, too silky, and she could see him almost visibly reining in his anger.

'You made me your wife, not your whore?' She arched with undue solemnity. 'And for that I should be grateful?'

She had to be mad, *insane*...and for one terrible

moment his eyes took on a frightening darkness, then became faintly hooded as he caught both of her hands in one of his.

'You want I should show you the difference?'

He reached out and flicked open the buttons of her evening jacket.

'Don't.' Defiance brought a flood of pink to her cheeks, and she attempted to pull her hands free without success.

The evening jacket came off, he reached for the zip fastening on her dress, slid it down and the garment slithered in a heap to the carpet.

Only her bra and briefs remained, and her eyes beseeched his as he undid the clasp, then stripped the briefs from her body.

'Duardo.' It was a plea, overlaid with instinctive fear.

His own clothes followed, first the jacket, his tie, then he freed his shirt buttons and shrugged the shirt off one shoulder, then the other, before tossing it onto the floor.

He loosened the belt on his trousers, undid the zip then toed off his shoes, his socks then stepped out of his trousers and tore the silk briefs free.

'You can't mean to do this,' she whispered as he pulled her close.

Then his mouth was on hers…hard, possessive, voracious and destructive as he plundered the soft inner tissues without care, using his tongue, his teeth to devastating effect.

It was like nothing she'd experienced…and never wanted to again. Ever.

If only that was all. Except it wasn't. She could see it in his eyes, the taut facial muscles assembling over bone, the grim line of his mouth.

It was then she began to fight in earnest, kicking out

with her feet, aiming to fasten her teeth on any part of his anatomy she could reach.

With no success whatsoever.

Her chest heaved from the exertion, and her breath came in gasps as he held her at arm's length.

Dear heaven. He couldn't...*wouldn't*. Surely?

For a long time he simply looked at her, and she stood mesmerized, unable to move in those few timeless minutes.

She could feel the tears begin to well behind her eyes and she blinked them back, willing them not to fall, for it would be the ultimate humiliation.

'Go to bed.' His voice was harsh. 'Before I do something regrettable.'

He released her and caught up his briefs, stepped into them then pulled on his trousers and tugged on his shirt.

Work. He needed to lose himself in graphs, figures, projections. Check emails, make calls.

Anything to remove his mind from the scene that had just taken place.

He turned and left the room, closing the door with an almost silent click, and went downstairs to seclude himself in front of a bank of computers. He brought up the screens and began checking data.

It was late when he closed everything down and quietly retraced his steps.

The bedroom was lit by one dimmed lamp on low, sufficient for him to see the large bed was empty. He scanned the room, saw clothes had been picked up.

He checked the *en suite*, then he turned down the bed, discarded his clothes, pulled on a robe and began checking the upstairs rooms.

Kayla wasn't in any one of them.

A faint chill settled deep in his gut. She hadn't left the house…the security alarm hadn't beeped an alert that any of the external doors had been opened.

Duardo descended the stairs and checked the kitchen, dining room, lounge, her home office. Dammit, the garage, each car.

There was only the media room remaining, and he crossed to it, saw the large screen was blank, the sound system off.

Where was she?

He was on the verge of leaving the room when something caught his eye. A faint movement, the slight swish of a tail.

And then he saw her. Curled up in a chair, her feet tucked beneath her, with the kitchen cat Maria usually kept in the laundry overnight comfortably settled on her lap.

Bright cat's eyes blinked at the intrusion, watching warily as he approached, and he soothed gentle fingers over its fur, lingered, then caught the animal's soft purr of appreciation.

'Sorry, little fellow,' Duardo murmured as he carefully dislodged and returned the soft ball of fur to its laundry bed.

He returned to the media room and stood looking down at her for what seemed an age. Then with infinite care he collected her into his arms and carried her upstairs to bed.

It was there, in the soft, muted lamplight, that he glimpsed the faint tracks of dried tears where they'd run unchecked on the edge of sleep.

The sight of them almost undid him, and he closed his eyes in silent self-castigation. A soft imprecation whispered from his lips as he laid her down between the sheets…and watched her body curl into a protective ball.

Por Dios.

He'd brought her to this? By his own hand, over a few wayward words tossed in anger?

Mierda.

With extreme care he slid down beside her and gently gathered her in. Felt her instinctive recoil as she came awake.

His lips teased her temple, then slipped down to settle at the edge of her mouth. 'Trust me, *querida*. And *feel*. Just…feel.'

He explored her lips, slipping in to soothe the swollen tissues with such incredible gentleness she almost wanted to cry.

His hands traced the delicate contours of her face, then slid to caress her shoulders, savoured the lingering perfume of the body lotion she favoured, then dipped low over her breast to take its sensitized peak into his mouth.

Something tore inside him as he felt her unbidden response, and he used his hands to cup her, shape the indentation of her waist, trace a path over her stomach. He felt it quiver beneath his touch, then he sought the heart of her femininity, gifting her the most intimate kiss of all.

Kayla closed her eyes and let her mind detach from her body, feeling it float to a place where she could examine the sensations he aroused, analyze and separate them from her heart.

She could feel the burgeoning sensuality, and she attempted to contain it…only to fail dismally as the familiar heat of orgasm coursed high, spiralling out of control as her body arched beneath his touch, bowed in exquisite suspension as she held on.

Then, after seemingly endless seconds, she gave in to the tactile nirvana he created, aware she had no choice as he sent her high again and again until she cried out her release and his mouth covered hers in a kiss that melted her bones.

There was the need for more. To feel him inside her, the long, slow thrust of his possession, and the silken fit as her inner muscles enclosed him.

He knew...how could he not?

A helpless groan emerged from her throat as he carefully positioned himself and slid slowly in to the hilt, paused there, then began to move, creating an age-old rhythm that brought them to the brink, held them there, then tipped them over in a glorious sensual free fall to a place where nothing else mattered.

Except them, and the emotion they shared.

If he wanted to impress the power he commanded over her, then he'd succeeded. In spades.

But that was all it was.

Sexual expertise.

The love they'd once shared no longer existed.

Survival meant accepting her life with Duardo *now*. Taking forward steps. Not looking backwards.

It was better for her health, welfare and state of mind.

Anything else was sheer folly.

Kayla slept, caught close against him, his lips buried at the edge of her temple.

CHAPTER NINE

IT WASN'T a big deal, Kayla silently assured herself as she entered the theatre foyer at Duardo's side.

Marlena in the lead role on stage posed no threat. And if by chance they mingled with selected guests backstage after the performance, there would be others present to defuse the tension.

Although Marlena was likely to be charm personified, providing an award-worthy act pretending friendship with the wife of one of her former consorts...*lover*, had yet to be determined.

It hardly mattered. There was no reason for it to hold any importance.

Yet it did. And Kayla was reluctant to explore *why*.

Mingling with fellow theatre-goers, indulging in social pleasantries provided a welcome distraction, and she was conscious of Duardo's close proximity, the sensual heat beneath the superb tailoring, the lurking sexuality that was his alone.

He had the power to affect her as no other man ever had...or ever would. Pheromones? Basic sexual chemistry, or something incredibly more profound?

There had to be a reason why two people were drawn

together, forsaking all others…because no one else could arouse quite the heightened degree of sensual magic that made it uniquely theirs.

The electronic buzzer summoned everyone to seek their reserved seating, and Kayla welcomed the dimmed lighting, the emergence of the orchestra, the curtain lifting to display the first scene, Act One.

The mastery of Shakespeare, the prose, sonnets…on occasion the subtle darkness in the hands of the costumed actors provided enjoyable entertainment. More, if one shared the cadence and expertise of the delivered word.

Kayla viewed the performance as a pleasant way in which to spend an evening. She was well aware to a Shakespearean buff it was whether the actor was worthy of the part, in comparison to the greats noted for their portrayals on some of the world's finest stages.

Was that the reason for Duardo's fascination?

Sadly she didn't know. There hadn't been the time or the opportunity to share such things.

Marlena, she had to admit, commanded a certain presence in the lead part. The actress's ability to *become* the character was truly an awesome transition, for during her time on stage she was so utterly convincing that no one, not even her worst enemy, could fault her.

Was it her acting prowess which drew Duardo's attention? Or did his fascination extend to her ability to portray any part a man might request in private…from the chaste virgin to the coquette, the innocent to the tart?

Certainly Marlena appeared to enjoy her role. So much so that, when the actress beseeched the audience, it appeared it was Duardo she directed her attention to.

A trick of the actress in the role of her character's

plight? Or a deliberate attempt to appear to be playing to Duardo alone?

Kayla told herself it hardly mattered…but it did. The thought Marlena might have been one of his intimates almost tore her apart.

Not only the actress, she decided shakily. *Any* woman.

She closed her eyes, then opened them again.

Give it a break. Reflecting on the past served little purpose, and changed nothing.

Focus on the stage production.

Sure, an inner voice derided. *That's easy when the lead actress's very presence is in your face.*

So…get over it.

It was something of a relief when the curtain closed at the end of the first act, and she met Duardo's slightly musing look as the lights came on during the short intermission.

'Marlena is very good in the part,' Kayla declared quietly, and saw his mouth curve a little.

'You sound almost surprised.'

She shot him a look of mild reproof. 'I'm attempting a sincere compliment.'

'Regarding her talent?'

'On the stage,' she qualified, and glimpsed the humour apparent in those dark eyes.

'Of course.'

He read her too well.

Did he know how often she fought with her emotions? The past vying constantly with the present? How in the darkness of night the line between love and hate was becoming increasingly hazy?

She wanted to be in control. Yet each day, each night it became more of a struggle for her to maintain a sense of distance.

Sharing good sex didn't equate to *love*.

And she couldn't afford to love him.

It was as well the lights began to dim, the orchestra resumed and the curtain lifted on the next act.

The ensuring hour and a half proved fascinating, and there was almost a sense of disappointment when the curtain fell on the final act.

Audience applause ensured the players took another bow, followed by a general exodus from the theatre.

'Marlena has invited a few friends to meet backstage.'

A refusal was impossible. Besides, she wouldn't give the actress the satisfaction of a no-show.

Smile-time, Kayla silently accorded, grateful she'd had plenty of practice in the social art.

There were security people, managers…who skilfully sorted bona fide guests from those hopeful of slipping through the security net undetected.

With Max in the background. His facial expression belying the cold stillness in those hard grey eyes. He resembled a predator, waiting, watching…for what?

Unbidden, a chill slithered down her spine.

Accolades were given, floral tributes delivered and the actress basked in the attention.

Not that any of it was undeserved, Kayla accorded silently. There were the congratulatory kisses…the light touch of lips to Marlena's cheek, the smiles, the laughter.

Including Duardo's salutation, for which the actress turned her head so his lips briefly touched her own.

Not such an innocent move, Kayla determined, noting the satisfied gleam evident in Marlena's eyes before it was quickly masked…and she was totally unprepared for the shaft of jealous pain lancing through her body.

To feel such a degree of anguish meant she had to care.

The knowledge hurt unbearably, for a one-sided love was no love at all.

With a tinkling laugh and a wave of her hand, the actress retreated into her dressing room to change.

Security staff began dispersing the crowd, with discreet invitations being given to selected guests to accompany the actress and some of the cast at an after-theatre party.

'Shall we join them?'

Kayla heard Duardo's drawled query, and sent him a steady look. 'Why not?'

Wisdom had nothing to do with her response. If she had a care for her emotional health or a modicum of common sense she'd have uttered a resounding *no*.

The venue was an upmarket inner-city restaurant lounge bar, where Marlena's people checked out the invited guests and provided a security escort to a private room.

Champagne flowed in abundance, finger-food was offered by uniformed waiters, background music filtered through speakers…and a selection of the city's theatre artistes mingled.

Marlena made the grand entrance half an hour later, exquisitely gowned, freshly made-up with not a hair out of place.

Her husband, obviously well-versed in his wife's *modus operandi*, quickly stepped aside to let Marlena take the limelight.

No matter there were other cast members present, Marlena was the *star*. In true diva form, she commanded attention and milked it for all it was worth. Each coquettish smile, the fluttering eyelashes, the expressive hand gestures…essentially performance-worthy, and geared towards the men present.

One man in particular.

Duardo Alvarez.

It was a game. One Marlena played for her own amusement, Kayla perceived. To provide an edge of excitement, mystery. A mischief-maker *par excellence*.

No doubt the actress saw Duardo's recently acquired wife as a challenge. The intrigue element already existed. Maybe if Marlena threw a few balls in the air, they might land where least expected.

The actress had already attempted one minor skirmish. Was she deliberately setting up the next one?

Kayla didn't have to wait too long to find out, and afterwards she had to examine whether she didn't unintentionally precipitate it by seeking the powder room.

There was a queue…isn't there always? The number of stalls allocated in such establishments were usually inadequate, and after taking her turn she crossed to the wide expanse of basins, used the soap and water then pulled down a paper towel.

'I was beginning to think you were joined to Duardo's hip.'

A quick glance in the mirror was all it took to see Marlena standing close by.

The actress's sultry purr set Kayla's teeth on edge.

'Perhaps he's joined to mine.'

'Oh, darling, don't delude yourself.'

She met the malevolent gleam in Marlena's eyes. 'Presumably you have a purpose?' Nothing like cutting to the chase.

'Duardo is—' the actress paused deliberately '—very important to me.'

'You imagine it's reciprocal?'

Marlena took a moment to examine her beautifully lacquered nails. 'He's a very *sexual* animal.' She glanced up and shot Kayla a vitriolic look. 'I doubt you're—'

'Enough for him?'

'Precisely, darling.'

'And you're more than willing to take up the slack?'

'Any time.'

The cat-like purr was back in evidence.

'Wouldn't your husband object?'

'We have an arrangement.'

'How—' it was her turn to use an effective pause '—interesting.'

'Darling, Max is gay. Where have you been?' The strange glitter was back in Marlena's eyes. 'Oh, of course. Working nine to five and waiting tables every night...for how long? Three years? Duardo's revenge must be very sweet, given he plotted your father's downfall and then chose to stand by and watch as you slipped deeper into poverty.' She sharpened figurative claws and homed in for the kill. 'Divine justice, darling, to have you abandon pride and grovel at his feet.'

Supposition was a dangerous thing... Hadn't Kayla been guilty of the same, only to discover she'd misjudged him?

There were occasions when silence was golden, and a dignified retreat even more effective.

Unfortunately, this wasn't one of them.

Kayla lifted her chin a little. 'Perhaps I *do* grovel well.' Her eyes sparked blue fire. 'But why *wife* when mistress would have sufficed?'

'Duardo's desire for an heir?'

Damn, she fell right into that one!

'As part of the perceived deal?' she countered with a deliberate lift of her eyebrows. 'Wrong, Marlena.'

Cut, and leave. *Now.*

For a moment she thought the actress might strike her, and she mentally reeled from the bitter acrimony evident in those dark eyes before Marlena turned away and made a flouncing exit from the powder room.

Dear heaven. It was possible to cut the tension with a knife.

She needed a few seconds to gather herself together before going back to the party. Lipstick, a few deep breaths, a practised smile and she emerged into the vestibule.

The temptation to keep walking and hail a cab home was difficult to resist. And she almost did. Except such an action would be a cop-out, and she was done with taking the easy route.

A hysterical bubble of laughter rose and died in her throat. *Easy?* She had money for the cab…but not the modem to free the front gates, the garage doors. Dammit, a key to any of the house doors. Nor did she have a clue how to disarm the security alarm.

It was past midnight. Maria and Josef would be in bed, ditto Spence.

'Are you OK?'

She didn't know whether to laugh or cry at the sound of that familiar drawl and the man who owned it…owned *her.*

'I'm perfectly fine.'

One eyebrow rose slightly. 'Uh-huh.' He touched a finger to the fast-beating pulse at the hollow beneath her throat. 'Cool, calm and collected.'

'I think I hate you.'

Duardo curled a hand round her chin and lifted it. 'Only *think?*'

Hot, angry tears threatened to cloud her vision, and she blinked rapidly to disperse them. 'Don't *play* me.' She couldn't fall apart. Not now, not here. Not ever, she decided fiercely.

He traced the edge of his thumb over her lower lip, felt it tremble and cupped her face. Her eyes were dark, so dark he could almost drown in them.

'Let's go. Home,' he added.

Kayla didn't offer so much as a word as the Aston Martin purred through the city streets, nor when Duardo garaged the car. Indoors, she made straight for the stairs, uncaring whether he followed her or not.

She wanted solitude. Preferably to sleep alone. In another bed, another room.

And she would, she determined as she entered their bedroom and crossed to her *en suite*.

The stilettos were the first to go, then the red silk chiffon evening gown with its fitted bodice and exquisite diagonally cut skirt.

Make-up removal took only minutes, and she released the pins from her hair, brushed its length and caught it into a loose pony-tail before pulling on a robe.

Duardo was in the process of undressing when she re-entered the bedroom, and she barely glanced at him as she moved towards the door.

'Where do you think you're going?'

She kept walking. 'Any room except this one.'

'You don't want sex…that's your prerogative. But we share the same room, the same bed.'

'You wish.'

He wanted to haul her in and kiss her senseless. Except it wouldn't solve a thing. 'Marlena. The powder room.'

'Brilliant deduction.'

He could imagine how it had gone. The very reason he'd gone looking for her when she was absent too long.

Kayla turned to face him, her expression tense, her eyes a shattering mix of blue fire and ice. 'I was going to walk out and get a cab. Except this…house—' she was darned if she'd refer to it as *home* '—is locked up like Fort Knox, and I don't have a key.' She drew in a deep breath and released it slowly. 'Marlena I can handle.'

'She's a temperamental diva. A very talented one who is contracted to a theatrical company in which I retain a financial interest.'

She got it. 'So it's in your best interests to play *nice*.'

'We share a professional relationship. That's all.'

The ice began to melt, but the blue fire remained. 'Perhaps you should tell her that.'

'I already did. Up front before she signed her first contract with me.'

'Well, there's the thing,' Kayla managed sweetly. 'Marlena doesn't appear to understand the boundaries.' She met the darkness in his eyes with silent mockery. 'Next you'll tell me she's a raving nymphomaniac who regards you as an ongoing challenge in between relationships.'

'That's a fairly accurate assumption.'

'Life should be so tough.' She turned back towards the door and pulled it open.

'The bedroom arrangement stays.'

'No.'

'You want to fight me?' His voice was a silky drawl that sent shivers scudding down her spine.

'Physically I could never win.' Even so, it wouldn't stop her from trying.

Duardo let her walk. She'd tire before he did, and while she slept he'd gather her up and bring her back where she belonged.

It was the early pre-dawn hours when he went searching for her, although she'd made no attempt to hide, as the room she'd chosen was only two removed from their own.

She looked so peaceful in the dim light reflected from the hallway, curled into a small, protective ball, her head burrowed against the pillow, hands tucked close to her chin.

For a moment he almost left her there. Except he wanted her with him, *there* beside him where he could reach for her. To place a possessive hand at her waist, a slender thigh, and bury his lips in the sweetness of her hair.

If he was careful she wouldn't stir. And if she did...he'd deal with it.

Kayla was lost in a dream, one where everything was good...so good she didn't want to leave it. Except a distracting shadow intruded where it had no place, and she murmured in protest as she fought off the return to reality.

Strong arms held her, and she could feel the heavy thud of a human heartbeat close to her cheek. Seconds later there was a shift in position, and she came sharply awake with the instant recognition of where she was and with whom.

'You don't play fair.' She balled a hand into a fist and threw a punch at his shoulder as he settled onto the bed and drew the covers over them both.

'Go to sleep.'

'You ruined my dream.' Her voice sounded faintly petulant even to her own ears.

He drew her in and settled her head against his chest. 'I can always provide you with another.'

'Emotional blackmail.'

'Sleep, *querida*.'

Amazingly, she did, and when she woke Duardo had already left for the city.

CHAPTER TEN

A NEW day inevitably held promise, and Kayla dressed in jeans, a singlet top, added a shirt and made it downstairs for a late breakfast.

It was a beautiful, clear day, the sun shone and there was barely a drift of cloud in an azure sky.

Spence appeared as she drained the last of her coffee.

'Ready whenever you are.'

'Five minutes.' She needed to collect her bag, laptop, cellphone, notes, suppliers' quotes…and apply lipstick.

'I'll bring the car around.'

She made it in six, and she checked her list as he headed towards Double Bay. The cottage should be cleared of stock, and she wanted to physically *see* the bare rooms, the better to visualize the designer's plans for fixtures and fittings. She also needed to confer with him on site, estimate refurbishment time, check stock arrival and placement, advertising and think about plans for the grand opening.

It made for a very busy morning, and it was Spence who called a halt for lunch.

Kayla picked up her cellphone and punched in a series of digits.

'I'll go grab something. Sandwiches? Any preference?'

'Chicken and salad. Bottled water. Thanks.'

He was back in ten minutes, and she took another ten as a break before reaching for her cellphone.

The designer arrived at three, and together they made a few minor adjustments to the plan. A sample box of votive candles, soaps and aromatherapy oils was delivered by courier, and at four Spence insisted on closing down for the day.

'I can manage another hour.' And still have time to shower, change and be ready for dinner.

'We have an appointment.'

A puzzled frown furrowed her forehead. 'Not that I recall.'

'Duardo's instructions. Collect what you need, I'll lock up and bring the rest.'

Everything. Swatches, samples, catalogues. Laptop.

'Where are we going?' The question seemed reasonable as Spence turned towards the city, instead of in the direction of Point Piper.

'We're almost there.'

A Porsche car dealership where a top-of-the-range silver four-wheel-drive stood waiting for her to claim.

'You're kidding me.'

Spence grinned at her disbelief. 'Yours. Unless you'd prefer another colour.'

Colour? The colour was just fine. 'I get to drive it home?'

'Perhaps a test run first?'

They did that, and it handled beautifully in spite of the fact she hadn't driven a vehicle for some time.

'You want to head out first, or shall I?'

'I'll follow you.'

It purred beneath her touch, all leashed power and class as she handled it through traffic and brought it to a smooth halt inside the garage.

Spence drew the Lexus in alongside, and handed her two modems together with two sets of keys.

'You'll need these.'

He collected samples, her laptop, and indicated he'd deposit everything in her office.

'Thanks for your help today. Everything. I really appreciate it.' She wrinkled her nose at him. 'And don't say you were just doing your job.'

She moved quickly upstairs, hit the shower then, towelled dry, she pulled on a robe. When she emerged into the bedroom Duardo was there in the process of discarding his clothes.

Her heartbeat immediately went into overdrive, visible in the pulse in the hollow of her throat, and she lifted a hand in an instinctive need to hide her body's wayward reaction to him.

'How was your day?' He emptied his pockets and placed his wallet and spare change on the valet frame.

'Busy. We achieved a lot.' Her eyes met his. 'Thank you for the wheels.'

'So…thank me.' His voice held a degree of musing mockery.

'I don't think we have time. Before dinner. I mean—' Oh, hell, she was digging herself into a deeper hole with every word! Worse, she could almost sense his silent amusement.

'Maybe a simple kiss will tide me over?'

'OK.' All she had to do was walk over to him, cup his face and bring it down to her own, then place her mouth on his.

Easy. *Simple.*

She should have known better.

The tentative kiss she offered didn't cut it, and she reached up on tiptoe, leaned in close then slid her tongue around his and drew it into her mouth. Savoured, explored and angled her head to gain better purchase.

Strong hands cupped her bottom as he lifted her against his hard-muscled frame, wrapped her legs around him and she held on, exulting in the feel of his arousal against the most sensitive part of her anatomy.

Its potent power robbed her of breath, and she groaned deep in her throat as his fingers sought the intimate heart of her, probed the highly sensitized clitoris and skilfully brought her to orgasm.

He plundered her mouth, swallowed her scream as she shattered and held her close as the intensity subsided.

'That wasn't fair,' she managed shakily.

His lips brushed her forehead and came to rest against her temple. 'How so?'

'All me, and not you.'

Kayla sensed his lips part a little, and imagined his smile.

'You want to miss dinner?'

It was a teasing game. Nothing more. And she entered into the spirit of it with a light laugh.

'And have Maria's efforts go to waste?' She pressed her lips to his, then drew back to regard him with mock severity. 'Besides, I'm hungry. For food.' Her eyes danced with wicked humour. 'Here's the plan. We'll go eat, indulge in polite conversation and you can anticipate what the night will bring.'

'In that case, go put on some clothes before I change your mind.'

He could, all too easily. He slid her down to her feet, saw the momentary indecision evident in those vivid blue eyes and pressed a light kiss to her lips.

'Go.'

Three years ago she would have given a seductive

laugh, caught hold of his hand and gone willingly into the shower with him. And they would have missed dinner without a second's thought, made love far into the night, snacked on food at some ungodly hour, then…

Don't go there. The words screeched silently inside head.

Love. Then it was love.

Now…it's just sex.

Was it too much to want him to shatter as she did and lose all sense of time and place…so there was only *her*? The one woman above all others who could take hold of his emotional heart and call it her own.

Kayla sought control, partially succeeding as she moved out of his arms and crossed to her walk-in wardrobe, selected clothes at random and began pulling them on.

Dinner was a convivial meal eaten out on the terrace overlooking the harbour. As they sampled Maria's fine cuisine the dusk began to shroud the landscape, turning colour to muted shades of silver and grey.

Streetlights flared and bright neon signs seemed more vivid against the night-time sky. Lit ferries glided through dark waters between the city and the northern suburbs, and the constant flow of traffic highlighted main arterial roads leading to and from the city.

It became a fairy wonderland Kayla would never tire of admiring.

But for how long? Duardo hadn't put a time limit on the length of their marriage. Her initial demand had elicited *as long as it takes*. Nor had he asked her to have his child.

Neither of which boded well for *ever after*.

It shocked her to acknowledge she wanted it all. His

love, fidelity…the gift beyond price mutually exchanged at their first wedding.

She'd meant it then, upheld it in her heart, her soul.

The question was…did he?

The knowledge that he might have disregarded it hurt unbearably, and she reiterated a silent vow to take each day, each night as it came, rather than agonise over the future and what it might hold. To do otherwise was madness.

'I distinctly recall you mentioned polite conversation.' Duardo's voice held indolent amusement, and she summoned a brilliant smile.

'Shall we begin with the mundane?'

'Work?' He sank back in his chair and regarded her thoughtfully. 'Meetings, phone calls, negotiations, mediating.' His shoulders lifted in a careless shrug. 'The usual.'

Kayla liked him like this. At ease, having exchanged a formal business suit for chinos and a chambray shirt. Relaxing at the end of the day over fine food and a glass of wine, with nothing more mentally taxing than sharing time with his wife on a beautiful early summer's night.

Yet even in relaxed mode, he bore the lithe strength of a warrior, the waiting, watchful quality of a man who'd seen much and weathered more in places no respectable person would frequent…where survival was the only game in town.

'You've reached a compromise with the shop fittings?'

Her features became animated as she replaced flatware and sank back in her chair. 'Just a few minor adjustments. It's all happening so fast. When the shop's done, maybe you'll come look it over?'

'Naturally.'

A faint smile teased her mouth as an idea came to mind. 'Maybe you'll let me test some of the samples on you?'

'You plan stocking supplies for men as well as women?'

'Select toiletries, oils.'

'This personal demonstration,' Duardo drawled. 'When do you envisage it taking place?'

She tilted her head a little. 'Tonight? If you're up to it, of course.' A mischievous gleam deepened her eyes. 'Shall we say nine-thirty? Your *en suite*?'

He rose to his feet. 'Done.'

An hour and a half later he entered the master suite to soft lighting, muted baroque music and the faint aroma of incense.

The bed was stripped to a covering sheet and layered with thick bath towels. A tray containing exotic shaped bottles was set on a bed pedestal, and Kayla stood wrapped in a towelling robe…waiting.

The door to his *en suite* was open, and steam drifted from the large bathtub.

'You get to remove your clothes.'

Duardo slanted an eyebrow. 'Does this personal demonstration allow you to remove them for me?'

'Definitely not.'

'Pity.' This was her game, and he'd play by her rules…for now.

Getting naked didn't take long, although he deliberately didn't hurry, and he turned towards her with a faintly quizzical smile. 'What next?'

'Please lie face down on the bed.'

He complied, with an animal-like grace that was uncontrived, and Kayla silently let out the breath she'd unconsciously been holding.

She knew every inch of his masculine body, each muscle flex, the strong bone structure. The small tattoo on one shoulder…the jagged keloid scar low on one hip flank.

The aromatic oil sample she chose held woodsy tones

and an element of musk, and she warmed it in her hands, then carefully massaged it in over his powerful shoulders, his arms, travelling towards his waist, hips, the tight curve of his butt, the muscular thighs.

He possessed a masculine beauty in size and muscular symmetry, honed by physical fitness, but not overstated or pumped. Just…lithe, powerful and all male.

She loved the feel of his body beneath her hands, its strength, and unbidden her hands slowed and lightly caressed…for how long? Surely only mere seconds?

Dear heaven, what was the matter with her? This wasn't meant to be seduction.

Dammit…what in hell are you *doing*?

The silent castigation never left her lips, and she forced her voice to sound normal.

'You can turn over now.'

Oh, my. The breath caught in her throat at the sight of his erection, and she almost chickened out. Except for a determined persistence to finish what she'd begun.

Start with his chest, and work your way down…way down, with scant attention to the part of his anatomy between his waist and the tops of his thighs.

Which was fine until she reached his waist, lingered over one hip, then the other, and heard the faint hiss of his breath as her hands slipped over the springy male hair couching the base of his penis and scrotum.

The temptation to tease and tantalize was paramount, but it would have only one end…and she wasn't done. Not yet. His arms and legs remained, followed by the bath.

The whole deal, not part of it.

His eyes remained closed, and when she had finished she capped the bottle of aromatic oil, then used a towel to wipe the excess oil from her hands.

'You can get up now.'

Kayla gasped in startled surprise as Duardo's hand encircled her wrist and tugged her close.

'If you ever use your hands quite like that on anyone else,' he intoned with dangerous silkiness, 'I can promise you'll live to regret it.'

His voice was a husky growl, and sensation arrowed through her body as she caught the dark intensity in his eyes, the flex of muscle and sinew as he sought control.

The tension was electric, and for a moment she couldn't move. Dared not, in case she invoked something she wouldn't be able to handle.

Her eyes remained locked with his, caught spellbound by an emotion she didn't want to define.

'There's the bath.' Her voice didn't even sound like her own. For the love of heaven, get a grip! 'Candles.' She was suddenly having trouble getting the words out. 'I need to light them.'

He released her hand, and she moved into the *en suite*, retrieved a taper with shaky fingers, lit and touched it to each wick in turn.

A delicate scent rose in the air, and she switched off the electric light, then turned to see Duardo standing in the aperture.

A lump rose in her throat, and she attempted to swallow it without visible effort. 'It's meant to be a total sensual experience.'

'For two, surely?'

'That's how it'll be promoted. I—merely want your reaction.' She was dying here. 'Opinion,' she corrected.

'Which won't be accurate if I bathe alone.' He moved in close and released the belt fastening her robe.

'I don't think—' She clutched the edges without success, and she cried out as he placed an arm beneath her knees and stepped into the bath.

The warm scented water closed over her as he turned her to face him.

He was too close, much too close, and her eyes widened as he picked up the sponge and placed it in her hand.

'This wasn't part of the plan,' Kayla began helplessly in a bid to wrest back some control.

'But you agree it can be adapted any which way?'

How difficult could it be?

Sure, a silent voice mentally derided. And who do you think you're kidding? Mere minutes ago *he* was the only one naked.

Now they both were.

So…soap the sponge, smooth the oil from his body…and leave.

She didn't linger, deliberately choosing not to meet his gaze as she dispensed the oil.

'It won't matter if there's some residue,' Kayla managed quietly. 'It's very good for your skin.' She replaced the sponge and began rising to her feet, except Duardo's hands curved over her shoulders, stilling her progress.

'Where do you think you're going?' His voice was dangerously soft, and her eyes widened as she sank down. 'My turn, hmm?'

The oil matched the scented candles, creating an ambience that was infinitely sensual, and she watched the steady flumes with a sense of fascination as he eased the soapy sponge over her silken skin.

It was sinfully erotic, the warm water, the scent, the candles. Being here with him.

His touch was slow, lingering at her breasts, shaping

and testing their weight as he brushed each tender peak with the edges of his thumbs.

They beaded beneath his touch, and her eyes dilated as piercing sweetness flooded the intimate heart of her. Myriad sensations coursed through her body, heating it with primitive hunger…for him, only him.

She wanted to cry out, but no sound emerged from her lips as he lifted her high…and held her as he used his mouth, his tongue, in an erotic tasting that had her clinging on to him as he took his fill. Urging her to the brink, until she shattered into a thousand splintering shards.

Then he positioned her carefully onto his rigid penis and eased into her, watching her body coalesce as she took him in to the hilt, briefly resting there before he began to move.

A heartfelt groan left her lips as she held on to him and enjoyed the ride, only to cry out as his mouth took possession of her own in a kiss that was so incredibly tactile she felt as if she'd lapse into serious meltdown.

Afterwards he tucked her head into the curve of his neck and held her, gently tracing the length of her spine in a soothing gesture.

Her hair was in disarray, and he thread his fingers through its silken length, easing it back behind each ear.

Like this, she could almost believe everything was right between them, and the past three years were a bad dream that had never happened.

If only.

In another lifetime…the one they should have had…there might have been a child by now. Surely that was what would have eventuated, even though the possibility had never been discussed?

Did a child form part of Duardo's agenda? A reason to

tie her to him in a loveless marriage? A legitimate successor to inherit his fortune and take it into another generation?

What if she was to share with him the fact that she'd accidentally missed taking a contraceptive pill?

A faint shiver shook her slim frame, and he moved, lifting her from him as he rose to his feet and stepped out from the bath with her in his arms, then he let her slide down to her feet and caught up a bath towel, wrapping it round her slim form before filching another for himself.

'On a scale of one to ten, the products deserve a ten.' He lowered his head to hers and captured her mouth in a brief, hard kiss. 'You,' he emphasised, 'were off the scale.'

'Thank you. I think.'

His lips formed a devilish curve. 'We could always arrange a repeat performance.'

Kayla swallowed compulsively. 'Not tonight.' Her emotions couldn't take it.

'When I return from New York.'

Her eyes searched his. 'When do you leave?'

'Tomorrow. Early. I'll be away a week.'

She wanted to ask to go with him. Except there was the boutique to organise, stock…

'I'll miss you.' The words slipped out, words she hadn't meant to say, and she felt the lick of heat course through her veins beneath the warmth of his smile.

Fool, she derided silently as she began extinguishing the candles and emptying the bath.

He finished with the towel, plucked hers and let both fall to the tiled floor. Then he curved a hand round hers and led her into the bedroom.

'Now for the soporific aftermath.'

A relaxed slide into somnolence.

She didn't think it would happen, for she didn't feel in the least tired.

Yet she drifted asleep within minutes of her head touching the pillow, oblivious to the man who lay quietly at her side.

CHAPTER ELEVEN

EACH day seemed more hectic as boxes of supplies were delivered and stacked in the back room of the boutique. Boxes Kayla quickly opened, checked the contents of against the stock-list, then quickly re-sealed to prevent fine builder's dust from infiltrating the packaging.

Carpenters worked widening the aperture between two distinct rooms, so they resembled one large, partially divided room. Then painters moved in, followed by the floor and wall tilers. When they finished, the shop-fitters delivered and fixed all the fittings in place.

Spence was there, overseeing operations, as he called it, and acting as go-for whenever needed.

Consequently Kayla rose early and drove to Double Bay each morning in time to allow the various tradesmen access into the cottage.

An hour's break around midday to catch up with Jacob, and she rarely arrived home much before dark. A shower, dinner, time on her laptop, late to bed…only to do it all over again the following day.

Duardo rang or sent an SMS each day in between meetings and negotiations…usually brief, given the time difference and their conflicting schedules.

The night hours were the worst, for it was then she'd turn over, reach for him in sleep… and discover an empty space in the bed.

She missed being held, his body's warm strength. Dammit, she missed *him*.

It was the reason she stuck to generalities and kept her voice light whenever they spoke on the phone. Glad he had no idea how the sound of his accented drawl curled round her heartstrings and tugged a little.

More than anything she wanted to sink into his arms and gift him her heart, her soul.

Except she didn't possess the courage.

Better to accept what he offered, and not wish for the unattainable.

Plans for the grand opening of the bathroom boutique were almost complete, the advertising organized. Invitations issued to browse were ready to be mailed, and tomorrow she'd put the general stock on display, create the special displays.

There were gift samples to assemble, and she decided each package would comprise a quality towelling washer, soap, a delicately fashioned bottle of aromatherapy oil and a small pouch of exquisite pot-pourri.

Tomorrow she'd purchase the sheer silk chiffon pouches, ribbons and tend to the gift samples.

Everything was falling into place, on schedule, and the excitement, the anticipation built with each passing day.

The boutique *had* to be a success. For many reasons, but uppermost was the need to prove her worth, to be able to repay Duardo the funds he'd supplied to set her up in business. It was a matter of pride, a measure of her integrity, and she determined not to fail.

Wednesday began as any other day, with an early breakfast, after which Kayla drove to the boutique and set to work on the special displays.

The stock she'd unpacked looked good on the shelves. Better than good, and the colours were beautifully co-ordinated.

She had a mental image of how the displays would look, and sketches to back them up.

It was midday when she broke for lunch, locked the cottage, grabbed a sandwich at a local deli. Then she went in search of pouches and ribbons needed for the gift samples.

Spence would check in around two, and with luck she'd manage to finish the special displays as well as package a number of samples by day's end.

'Soon,' Kayla promised as Spence tapped his watch and declared *time*. 'You go on ahead. I'll call in to see Jacob, and be home by eight.'

'I'll stay.'

'Why? There's no need.'

His pleasant features assumed a serious expression. 'Duardo—'

'I'll be behind locked doors, my car is parked round the corner, I carry a personal alarm, and—' she paused for effect '—you're forgetting I walked from the railway station to my flat late at night *every* night for more than two years.' She gestured with her hands. 'I'll be fine.'

'Call me when you're ready to leave the hospital.'

'Promise. Now go.'

She locked the door behind him, pulled down the new shade and set to work. Another hour, and she'd be well ahead. What was more, she'd call Jacob, put the cellphone on loud-speaker and chat for a while in lieu of stopping by.

Kayla hadn't long cut the call to Jacob when her cellphone rang and she picked up, heard Duardo's voice, felt the warmth pool deep within and leant against the new counter. 'Hi.'

'How is the cottage shaping up?'

Business. OK, she could do that. 'Really well.' She relayed the current rundown in brief. 'What about things on your end?'

'Tense.'

His negotiation skills were legendary. 'You're playing hardball.'

His soft laugh played havoc with her nerve-ends. 'Tactics.'

The sudden blast of a car-horn street-side provided a momentary intrusion.

'You're not driving?'

His query was sharp, and she was quick to assure, 'It's outside.'

'Outside *where*?' His voice was quiet…almost too quiet.

'The cottage.'

'Put Spence on.'

Oh, hell. 'He left ahead of me.'

'On your instructions?'

There was no point denying it. 'Yes.'

'Lock up and leave.'

Her fingers tightened on the cellphone. 'Excuse me?'

'Do it.'

'You're being unreasonable.'

She could almost hear him reining in his anger. 'Kayla—'

'OK. Consider it done.' She didn't wait for his response, and cut the connection.

Damn his arrogance. She was almost inclined to ignore his dictum by remaining another half-hour, just for the hell of it.

Except she wouldn't put it past him to call Spence, and no way was it fair he should take any of the blame.

However, she picked up a silk pouch, added a pot-pourri sample, towelling washer, soap and aromatherapy oil. Then she looked at the five assembled piles comprising her quota for the day, and assembled a few more. Tomorrow would see them done, then she could begin with the ribbons.

Just then her cellphone rang, and she checked caller ID, swore softly and picked up. 'I'm on my way. Seriously,' she assured Spence, and reluctantly collected her bag, checked the external doors, set the alarm and locked the main door behind her.

The early-evening café society crowd was beginning to fill the pavement tables, and she resisted the temptation to order a latte and sit awhile. Instead, she ordered a latte to go.

Summer daylight-saving was in force, and it was good to feel the sun's warm rays on her skin as she walked to where the Porsche was parked.

Once darkness fell it would become cool, but for now the promise of summer was in the air, the azure sky clear and there was a feeling of satisfaction she'd put in a productive day's work.

Someone bumped into her, and she almost lost her footing, then he was gone.

Definitely a *he*, and young by the fluidity of his gait, although it was impossible to tell for sure, with the hood of his jacket covering the back of his head.

Kayla shrugged her shoulders and crossed to the Porsche, delved into her bag for the key and alarm modem…and felt something warm trickle down her arm.

Blood?

From where?

When she looked, her singlet top bore a long slice across a lower rib. Blood welled and seeped into the cotton from a nasty-looking gash. It was then she felt the sting of pain.

What on earth? That silly idiot had slashed her with a knife. He hadn't tried to snatch her bag. So…*why*?

She grabbed a handkerchief from her bag and held it against the wound in an effort to stem the flow of blood.

At that moment Spence drew alongside in the Lexus and leapt out from behind the wheel.

'The cavalry has arrived.'

'Not before time.' He took one look, then whipped out a handkerchief of his own and compressed it against the wound. 'It needs sutures.' He took the keys and modem from her hand, checked the Porsche then led her to the passenger side of the Lexus. 'In you get.'

He took her to a private hospital, sat with her while the doctor sutured the wound then he phoned in a report to the police, made a second call, talked quietly and handed Kayla the cellphone.

'Duardo.'

Charming. Just what she needed…the third degree. 'I'm fine,' she said without preamble.

'Debatable.' His voice was icily calm, and brought goose-pimples to her skin. 'The medic will prescribe pain-killers and something to help you sleep. Take them, *querida*.' He paused fractionally. 'Spence will fill you in on the rest.'

'He can't *do* this,' Kayla vented an hour later as she pushed a plate of partly eaten food to one side, her appetite gone.

'It's as good as done,' Spence assured quietly. 'Notices will be printed, ready to be mailed out late tomorrow.

Posters will be fixed to both cottage windows and affixed to the door announcing a two-week delay in opening.'

'But—'

'No *buts*.'

'He's being ridiculous.'

'Protective.'

Kayla's eyes sparked with blue fire. 'Ridiculous.'

'You can tell him so tomorrow.'

'What do you mean...*tomorrow*? He's not due back until Sunday.'

Spence checked his watch. 'He's boarding a flight around now.'

'Whereupon his arrival will cause the shit to hit the fan,' she deduced, and glimpsed the faint humour evident in his gaze.

'Inelegantly put, but an accurate assumption.'

'It was merely a random action,' she opined with a careless shrug. 'Could have happened to anyone any-where.'

'Except you're the wife of an extremely wealthy man, familiar to many via recent media coverage,' Spence re-layed quietly. 'Therefore more vulnerable than most. Hence the reason certain protective measures are in place.'

Which she'd chosen to ignore. He couldn't, wouldn't alarm her with the rest. Investigative suspicions were due for confirmation any day soon.

Her eyes clouded. 'You think the attack was deliber-ate?'

'There are those who know Duardo is out of the coun-try.'

'And he has enemies?'

Stupid question.

Any man who'd hauled himself off the streets as a

youth and made a fortune had to have engineered some high-risk deals. Envy and jealousy had the power to become volatile in the minds of some. Men who'd felt wronged...women slighted.

Spence appeared to choose his words. 'Shall we say his absence provides a window of opportunity to get to him through you?'

You're wrong, she managed silently. I'm merely someone he's sought to avenge for wronging *him*. He doesn't *care*.

What she needed, Kayla decided, was a long, commiserating chat with someone who *did* care. 'I'll go call Jacob, take a shower then hit the bed.'

Spence retrieved a small packet and placed it in her hand. 'A measured dose of painkillers and a sleeping pill. Take them when you're ready to go to sleep.'

The shower helped ease some of the tension, and she lingered far longer than necessary, enjoying the warm, pulsing water, the scented body-wash. Then, dry, she pulled on a towelling robe, collected her cellphone and propped herself up in bed.

Jacob answered on the third ring, recognised something in her voice and demanded, 'What's wrong?'

Kayla relayed minimum facts, offered reassurance and slid straight into active listening mode.

'Why do you think Duardo is already on his way home?'

'To bawl me out in person,' Kayla offered, and heard her brother's 'tsk tsk' in response.

'Do you ever wonder why he married you?'

Every day. 'Because he could call the shots.'

'Not that he might never have stopped caring?'

'Oh, sure. Like that's a possibility.' And it snowed in summertime!

'Any fool could see you shared something special.'

It felt as if something tore inside her heart. 'Maybe. *Then.*'

'Our father was a pompous ass.'

'Hey,' she chastised. 'Don't speak ill of the dead.'

'He wanted to keep us to himself. I wasn't old enough for it to matter. But you were. And he ruined your life.' There was a pause for breath. 'Then he pulled the plug on his own, and left you to pick up the pieces.'

'That's harsh judgement.'

'But true.'

She hesitated, then offered slowly, 'I pegged Duardo's motivation as revenge.'

'Maybe you're wrong.'

'I don't see how I can be.'

'Because he waited for you to approach him?' She didn't answer, and Jacob went on, 'There was every chance he'd turn you away. But he didn't.'

Yet he stipulated conditions. And put Spence on my tail.

'He's given back everything you had.'

Except his love.

'He's postponed the shop opening,' she protested.

'Sensible, given you'll need to provide police statements and recuperate. Not to mention allow for the aftershock element.'

'Oh, for heaven's sake,' Kayla extrapolated. 'Don't you get on the "fragile flower" bandwagon, too!'

'It's good to know you're being well taken care of.'

She was, but that didn't make it any easier.

'Get some sleep, sis,' Jacob bade gently. 'And don't *think* too much. Ring me in the morning. Promise?'

'OK. Goodnight.'

Kayla checked the time, saw it was just after ten, and she filled a glass with water and swallowed down the pills Spence had given her.

The pain wasn't too bad, but her mind was too active for easy sleep.

How long before the pills took effect?

Maybe if she read for a while…

She picked up a book and read two pages, and that was the last thing she remembered until she woke the next morning, stretched then gasped in pain.

Wound. Sutures. Images flooded her brain in a flash, and she slid carefully from the bed, crossed to the *en suite* then began pulling on clothes.

Breakfast, then more painkillers, and she'd be ready to face whatever the day would bring.

Maria fussed over her like a mother hen, Josef enquired about her health and Spence was so solicitous it almost made her weep.

Kayla chose to eat on the terrace, and called Jacob while she sipped a second cup of coffee. The police arrived at nine, asked numerous questions, took her statement and left more than an hour later.

Lunch came and went, and she waved aside any suggestion she should rest. What she needed, she decided, was something to do.

Time spent in her home office would suffice. She could double-check stock, anticipate sales and precipitate new orders. She also needed to check the time margin between order and delivery…if she should prepare for any hiccups. She didn't want to run short of anything. When it came to luxury items, clients tended to want them at once…not have to wait for orders to come in.

It was there Duardo found her, and he stood drinking in the sight of her as she sat head bent over the laptop screen.

Conflicting emotions tore at him, and he controlled them with effort.

She *looked* fine. A little pale, and he hoped she'd slept better than he had during the long flight home. He'd caught a cab from the airport and spent the entire time on his cellphone, checking with Spence re his investigative process. Then he made a few calls to certain unlisted numbers and called in a few favours.

If his suspicions were correct… It would take time, but the unravelling process had begun within minutes of Spence taking Kayla to hospital.

The faint click of the door closing caught her attention, and she looked up, met his dark gaze and held it as he crossed to her desk.

'What do you think you're doing?'

His presence was a formidable force, and she sensed the tension emanating from his powerful frame.

'Hello to you, too.'

'Close the programme down and shut the laptop.'

'Bite me.'

He didn't move, but she felt the lethal intent barely held in restraint. 'You have no idea how close I am to doing just that.'

All day she'd anticipated this moment, and she'd become increasingly wound up with each passing hour. 'There was no need for you to rush back. I'm fine. Really.'

'Sure you are. Those dark circles beneath your eyes are simply a figment of my imagination.'

'Maybe you should take a look at your own.'

A muscle bunched at the edge of his jaw. 'Shall we start over?'

'Aim for polite neutrality?'

Duardo moved round the desk, leant forward, pressed the *save* key on the laptop then closed the screen.

'Don't—'

'I just did.'

He was too close, too male…too *much*. If he touched her, she'd fall to pieces.

For a long moment she bore his appraisal, refusing to bow beneath it, then her eyes flew wide as he cupped her face and lowered his mouth to hers in a slow, gentle kiss that almost tore her apart.

When he lifted his head she could only look at him with tear-drenched eyes, and she veiled them, afraid of what he might see.

With care he drew her to her feet, caught her hand in his and led her from the room.

'Duardo—'

'I need a shower and a change of clothes.'

'And that involves me…how?'

'For a start, you can hush that sassy mouth.'

He crossed into the foyer and made for the stairs. When he reached their suite he drew her inside and closed the door.

Kayla watched as he discarded his jacket, dispensed with his tie and the rest of his outer clothing.

'Five minutes, hmm?' With that he crossed to his *en suite*. Seconds later she heard the hiss of water, glimpsed the escaping steam…and knew she shouldn't stay.

To remain quiescent, *waiting,* seemed the height of folly. Except her limbs didn't want to obey the dictates of her brain.

Fool. If you leave, he'll only come after you, and that won't help at all.

She crossed to the splendid antique dresser and moved the baccarat crystal ornament, looked at it with an analytical eye then slid it back to its original position.

Her stomach felt as if a dozen butterflies had invaded it and were desperate to escape.

You and me, both!

Go. Stay. What a mess of contradiction. So go look at the view outside the window. Anything. But *do* something.

She moved restlessly to the wall of glass, heard the shower cease and endeavoured to focus on the clean-cut symmetry of the lawn, the garden borders alive with flowers and the small, carefully pruned shrubbery.

The water in the tiled pool shimmered beneath the sun's rays, and she watched a bright-plumed parrot coast in to perch on the edge of the bird-bath, drink from the water, look around then spread its wings and fly to settle high in the branches of a large tree.

She sensed rather than heard Duardo cross the room and stand behind her, then his hands curved over her shoulders.

His warm breath teased tendrils of hair close to her temple, and heat coursed through her veins as his lips settled against the curve of her neck.

'Come lie with me, hmm?'

'It's the afternoon,' Kayla protested.

'What's that got to do with anything?'

'You should sleep.'

'I will. Soon.' He turned her round to face him, and she couldn't read anything from his expression. The towelling robe moulded his muscular shoulders, the broad chest, and accented his narrow waist.

'But first,' he began as he reached for the buttons on her blouse. 'I need to see—' He freed the last button and pushed the fine cotton edges aside. A sterile gauze pad covered the wound, and he carefully eased the lower tapes free.

It wasn't deep, but the blade's tip had sliced sinew and touched bone at her ribs.

She knew what it looked like. Betadine, sutures, slightly swollen, puckered skin. The wound would heal, the swelling subside, and in time a fine white line would be all that remained.

His eyes blazed with a primitive dark savagery, and he said something vicious beneath his breath before carefully pressing the tapes back in place.

'You have to know I'll tear everything apart until I find who did this.'

Kayla felt the breath catch in her throat, and the beat of her heart went into overdrive.

She could almost feel sorry for the culprit. It was on the tip of her tongue to say it could have been worse. Except one glance was all it took to realise he was already three steps ahead of her, that having endured long hours on the flight had done little to ease his rage.

As she would have been, if the situation had been reversed.

For a few timeless seconds she stood frozen, unable to move if her life depended on it.

No one could feel quite this degree of anger…if they didn't *care*.

Could Jacob possibly have it right? The mere thought made her head spin.

Whoa. Going there wasn't good for her peace of mind.

Dammit, Duardo hadn't *said* anything.

But then, neither had she.

A hand cupped her chin and tilted it. 'Want to talk about it?'

About *what*? How much I love you? How I never really stopped? And…*do you love me*?

Like that was going to help!

'You didn't have to cut short your trip.' That was safe, ordinary.

'Yes,' he said quietly. 'I did.' His hands slid over her face and buried themselves in her hair. His head descended and his mouth captured her own, angled and went in deep with such exquisite gentleness she sank in against him and let him feast.

He began lightening the kiss, felt her soundless moan and gradually lifted his head. With infinite care he eased her blouse free, then undid the clasp of her bra before moving to the snap on her jeans.

'Please—'

'Patience, *querida*.' He traced a finger along the waistline of her jeans, felt her stomach quiver then lowered the zip fastening.

Dear lord. She was going up in flames, and he'd hardly touched her.

He eased the jeans down over her hips, let her step out of them, dispensed with her briefs then led her towards the bed.

With one fluid movement he tossed back the covers and drew her down onto the sheets, shrugged out of his robe and joined her.

Kayla searched for something flip to say, but the words didn't find voice as he brushed his lips to her shoulder.

'Indulge me, *querida*. I so badly need to do this.'

He began tracing a path to her breast, savoured its peak, teased its twin then trailed down to caress the indentation at her navel.

She thread her fingers through his hair and held on as he travelled low, seeking the moist labia, tracing the folds with the tip of his tongue before unerringly finding the sensitized clitoris.

Involuntarily she arched against him and he held her hips, laving the warm moistness until she cried out and begged for release…then soothed her as she came.

Earth-shattering, explosive…more, so much *more* than she'd ever experienced as he recaptured her heart, her soul.

Emotional tears welled and spilled to run in slow rivulets down each cheek as she lay there bare…so utterly bare, and wholly *his*.

As she had always been. Always would be.

Did he know?

Dear God, how could he *not* know?

Her body shook slightly as he trailed light kisses over her stomach, then traced a slow path to the hollow at the base of her throat before settling over her mouth in a slow, evocative kiss.

She shaped his face with her hands, and kissed him back, loving him with her mind, the touch of her lips…until he reluctantly lifted his head and reached for the bedcovers.

'Stay with me, *querida*.'

He drifted into sleep within minutes, and she lay at his side until the sun's light faded and dusk became dark.

CHAPTER TWELVE

It was a beautiful morning, the sun's warmth already evident as they lingered over coffee on the terrace.

Kayla poured a second coffee, then she sank back in her chair and viewed the man seated opposite.

Duardo looked refreshed and incredibly vital after a good night's sleep, and sharing breakfast with him on a weekday was a bonus. Somehow she'd expected him to follow his usual pattern and leave early for the city. But he was here, apparently not in any hurry…and it was nice.

Another concession to her knife attack?

Last night had been something else. Just thinking about his intimate supplication brought a flood of heat pooling deep inside, and she involuntarily shifted a little to contain the involuntary spasm spiralling through her body.

He had to know how he affected her…how could he not?

She spared him a glance, and almost died at the brooding passion evident in those dark eyes…then it was gone.

'Finish your coffee,' he indicated with indolent ease. 'You need to pack. Spence is driving us to the airport in an hour.'

She looked at him in disbelief. 'You're joking, right?'

'We're taking a late-morning flight to Brisbane, then driving to Noosa.'

'There's a reason?' She paused deliberately, then offered, 'Other than the obvious one?'

Duardo lifted an eyebrow. 'Meaning?'

'Moving me out of town.'

'You object to spending the next few days in my company?'

'Queensland? *Noosa*? Sunshine, sandy beaches, top restaurants…what's not to like?'

'That wasn't the question.'

'I guess having you along won't be a hardship,' she conceded and witnessed his mocking smile.

'*Gracias.*'

Her eyes gleamed with wicked humour. 'Don't mention it.'

'An hour, Kayla,' he reminded as he ascended the stairs at her side.

'We're talking beachwear, something suitable to wear to dinner?'

'Casual.'

OK, she could do that.

Kayla made it with a few minutes to spare, and she slid into the Lexus as Spence deposited both bags in the rear compartment.

The flight to Brisbane was uneventful, and on arrival Duardo organised a hire car.

It was years since she'd last visited the Sunshine Coast, and the changes were many, with numerous resorts, apartment buildings and boutiques.

Magical, and she said so as they rode the lift to the penthouse apartment in one of the very modern buildings overlooking the ocean on Hastings Street.

Exquisitely furnished, it was a multi-million-dollar dream with two bedrooms, each with an *en suite*, a study, lounge and ultra-modern kitchen, offering magnificent ocean views.

'It's beautiful,' she complimented with utter sincerity.

'Thank you.'

'Another of your acquisitions?'

He inclined his head. 'The building has only recently been completed, and now seemed a good opportunity for a personal inspection.'

Why should she be surprised? His entrepreneurial skills were well-known.

'So we get to unpack, change into casual clothes, wander Hastings Street, find a restaurant and eat dinner?'

'Sounds like a plan.'

They began with a stroll along the boardwalk fronting the beach, chose *Sails* restaurant, nestled at the far end where the boardwalk finished and the side-street began.

Lovely ambience, great food and fine wine completed a relaxed evening, and Kayla said as much as they returned to the penthouse.

It would have been so easy to say 'I love you' as Duardo undressed her and took her to bed. Except the words remained locked in her heart, unable to find voice.

One day melded into another as they rose when they felt like it, took breakfast at a different restaurant each morning, explored the shops, the boutiques, spent a day driving to the Glasshouse Mountain, Montville, Maleny...beautiful country, lush green hills and quaint villages with numerous craft shops.

There were times in the apartment when Duardo plugged in the laptop and she settled herself in a comfortable chair, leafed through a magazine, read or watched television.

The nights were something else. Nights she didn't want to end, or the loving to change.

It was almost as if the past three years didn't exist, and Kayla experienced a sense of reluctance as Sunday dawned and they took the late-afternoon flight home.

Tomorrow Duardo would return to the city, and she felt strangely restless, wanting, *needing* to do something constructive.

The bathroom boutique was an addictive lure, and she wanted so badly to go check it out.

'Just for an hour or two,' Kayla pleaded as Duardo drank the last of his coffee over breakfast next morning.

'No.'

'I'll ensure Spence stays with me.'

'That's a given, wherever you go.'

'Bodyguard duty?'

His eyes speared hers. 'Until whoever is responsible for injuring you is behind bars.' His voice was hard, inflexible...dangerous.

He rose to his feet, shrugged into his suit jacket, crossed round the table and settled his mouth on hers in a possessive kiss, then he collected his briefcase and laptop. 'Take care.'

OK, so she'd spend an hour or two in her home office, call on Jacob and have Spence deliver her home in time to shower and change for dinner.

'This is definite overkill,' Kayla evinced as Spence negotiated the Lexus through heavy late-afternoon peak-hour traffic.

'One slip was bad enough. There won't be another.'

She had to ask, 'Any development in the investigation?'

'A lead. Duardo has access to contacts—'

'The police can't or won't use,' she concluded in shrewd summation.

'You could say that.'

Dinner was a pleasant meal, in that Maria served one of Kayla's favoured dishes, followed by an exquisite dessert. The caring thought touched her tender heart, and she made the impulsive decision to gift the housekeeper a complete bathroom package from the boutique.

Duardo took his coffee into his home office, and Kayla settled comfortably into a chair in the media room and slotted in a DVD. When the credits rolled, she closed the set and went to bed, read for a while then fell asleep.

It was an hour later when Duardo entered the room, and he took in her peaceful features—the cream-textured skin, the soft mouth—and felt his body tighten with need.

She was beautiful. Inside, where it mattered most, with a strength of character. Values…and pride.

So much pride, there were times when he wanted to wring her slender neck.

Yet he identified with it…admired, even as he cursed the quality. For it was a quality he also possessed.

A tenacity to succeed against all odds.

He banked down a surge of anger that anyone would choose to harm her…for whatever reason. Soon, very soon, he'd have the answers. And when he did, the person responsible would be consigned to their own private hell.

It took only seconds to discard his clothes and slide into bed beside her. She didn't stir, and he closed the bedside lamp, then settled down to sleep.

The insistent peal of a cellphone intruded on Kayla's subconscious, and she slid up against the pillows as Duardo activated the call.

It was late. Really late. Who on earth could be ringing at this hour?

'Yes.' Duardo's voice was deep, clipped. 'Of course. I'm on my way.'

'What's wrong?'

It was inevitable she'd ask, and he slid out of bed, walked naked across the room and hurriedly pulled on briefs, jeans and a T-shirt.

'I'll be gone awhile. Go back to sleep.'

'Sure. And I can do that easily, not knowing where you're going or why.'

She'd discover the truth soon enough, and better she heard it from him.

'That was the police. There's been a fire.'

Her face paled and her eyes widened into huge dark sapphire pools. 'Not the boutique?'

He stepped into trainers and fixed the laces. 'Yes.'

'I'm coming with you.'

She was already out of bed and pulling on underwear.

'The hell you are.'

She reached for jeans, pulled on a T-shirt and raked fingers through her hair. 'Try and stop me. I'm with you, or following you. Choose.'

'Kayla—'

She slid her feet into trainers, then filched the keys to the Porsche from a drawer. 'Choose, dammit!'

Duardo caught hold of her wrist. 'Give them to me. I'll drive.'

The acrid smell of smoke was in the air as they reached Double Bay, and she saw the revolving red lights atop two fire-trucks as they turned into the street. Two police cars, blue and red lights flashing, were positioned to provide a traffic block.

'Stay here.'

'No way in hell.' She was out of the seat the instant he cut the engine.

'Move one inch from my side, and I'll haul your sweet ass into the car and lock it.'

'My ass?'

'The car.'

Kayla shot him a dark look. 'Got it.'

He caught her hand in his, and she didn't think to remove it.

One glance was enough to determine the firefighters had the blaze under control. Long, thick hoses snaked across the road, and there was water everywhere.

Voices rang out in the night air, the words mostly indistinguishable, and uniformed police conferred with whoever was in command of the fire.

Duardo identified himself, *her*, and listened as a detective reported an update on the incident.

'The twenty-four-hour security you posted on the building paid off. A youth was caught running away from the scene. We have him in custody.'

Kayla tuned out, and did her best to check the damage from her vantage point.

It didn't look good beneath the floodlights illuminating the scene. The cottage windows were black from smoke, half the roof appeared to have fallen in and she could have wept at the state of the stock…what, if anything, was left of it.

Everything took on a blur-like quality as statements were given, information supplied and Duardo conferred with his private security.

Yellow crime-scene tape was placed around the cottage, one fire-truck pulled away, closely followed by a police car.

'Let's go.'

Duardo led her to where he'd parked the Porsche, and she climbed into the passenger seat, fixed the seat belt in place then looked at him in silent askance as he captured her face and fastened his mouth over her own in a kiss that was many things.

Possessive, frankly sensual and hopelessly flagrant.

'What was that for?' Kayla demanded helplessly when he lifted his head.

'Distraction.'

'It didn't work.'

He clipped his belt in place, ignited the engine and headed home.

She looked sightlessly out the windscreen. 'Who would do such a thing?'

'If the youth in custody is also responsible for injuring you, it won't take long to get him to name whoever paid him.' He'd make sure of it. And if the lead he already had was proven…

She felt numb with shocked emotion.

So much vengeance. Aimed at *her*. Why? Because Duardo had made her his wife? It didn't make sense. But then the actions of someone possessed of an unstable mind rarely made sense…except to those trained in psychiatry.

There was nothing she could think of to say, and she sat in silence during the short drive home.

Duardo took one look at her strained features as they entered the bedroom and swore softly beneath his breath.

'*Querida*. Bed, hmm?'

Her dark eyes were dilated with delayed shock as she turned towards him. 'I needed to see it for myself.'

He caught hold of her hand and brought it to his lips.

'Bricks and mortar, timber. Stock. It can be replaced. All of it.'

'But it was my stock.' My dream. The work, the magic...gone.

He undressed her, discarded his own clothes, slid into bed and gathered her in, then held her until she slept.

CHAPTER THIRTEEN

KAYLA swore softly beneath her breath when her cellphone rang, and she automatically picked up and identified herself.

Two days had passed since the cottage fire...days she'd spent secluded in her home office, accessing data for insurance purposes, tending to police procedure, redrawing plans. It was too soon to gain building quotes, as no one was allowed on site.

The paperwork kept her busy, occupied her mind and helped prevent her *thinking* too much.

'Kayla?'

The sound of her name brought her sharply into the present.

'Spence will bring you into my office.'

Duardo, sounding incredibly *formal*. Why?

'Now?'

'Yes, now.'

She heard the soft click as he cut the connection.

Well. No hello, no goodbye... She had half a mind to call him back and tell him to go jump.

In fact, she was about to hit speed-dial when there was a knock at her office door.

Maria? Josef? Spence?

She crossed the room and pulled open the door.

Spence.

'I have the Lexus out front.'

'Just like that? No questions asked, no answers given?'

'Duardo intimated the matter is urgent.'

'So I gather.' She threw him an exasperated look. 'I'll go grab my bag.' It took only minutes before she slid into the front seat beside him. 'This had better be good.'

They made the city without hitting too many traffic snarls, and Spence swung the Lexus down into the underground car park beneath Duardo's office building, parked then accompanied her in the lift to the high floor housing Duardo's suite of offices.

Whereupon there was instant recognition from the girl on Reception, followed by the appearance of Duardo's PA.

'They're waiting for you.'

They?

A minute later they were ushered into Duardo's office, and Kayla's eyes dilated at the sight of the woman seated opposite him.

Marlena.

Kayla watched as Duardo rose to his feet and crossed the room to her side, lowered his head and brushed his mouth against her own.

In silent apology for his brusque summons?

Spence remained standing just inside the closed door. The entire scenario was seriously weird.

'Really, *Duardo*,' the actress said in reproof. 'Our business affairs hardly need the presence of your—' she paused deliberately '—wife. Or your major-domo.'

He caught hold of Kayla's hand, linked his fingers

through her own and brought them to his lips. 'But they do,' he offered smoothly.

'I wish you'd move it along, darling. You've kept me waiting almost half an hour. I've read the new contract, it's fine. Why don't I sign it, your PA can witness my signature and I'll leave?'

'Because I'm withdrawing the contract, and declaring it null and void.'

'I beg your pardon?'

He turned slightly and filched duplicate copies of a thick document from his desk, released Kayla's hand and tore the pages in half, then in half again and tossed them into the waste-paper bin.

'Have you gone mad?'

Very much in *diva* mode, Kayla noted with interest as Duardo took hold of her hand again.

What in hell was going on here?

'Maybe I can jog your memory,' Duardo declared with dangerous silkiness. 'Bryan McIntyre. Two thousand dollars. Your instructions to harm my wife.'

She had to hand it to Marlena...the actress didn't so much as blink.

'I have no idea what you're talking about.'

'Five thousand dollars. The deliberately lit fire in my wife's boutique in the dead of night.'

'For heaven's sake. You can't possibly believe—' She pressed a hand to her heart in horror. 'We're *friends*. More than friends. I couldn't—'

'But Max did.'

'He may have meddled—' A hand fluttered eloquently. 'He enjoys a little mystery.'

'It was Max who let Jacob's debt at the casino ride and accumulate.' Duardo's voice held a lethal silkiness. 'Max who orchestrated Jacob's beating with instructions to break his leg.' Each word fell with damning truth. 'Kayla's attack. The fire.'

'Max wouldn't do that!'

'The police have him in custody.'

'*No*. I'll sue—'

'My line, I think. Bryan McIntyre was found at the scene of the fire and taken into custody. He's been singing like a canary in an effort to protect his own skin.'

Marlena rose to her feet. 'I don't believe you.' She turned towards the door. 'I'm leaving. You'll never hear from me again.'

Spence didn't move, and Kayla watched as the actress turned to face Duardo.

'Tell your *henchman* to step aside.'

He wasn't done.

'Max's bank and telephone records have been accessed. Bryan McIntyre's prints were found on a tin of flammable liquid discarded at the scene of the fire. His confession is sufficient to convict you.'

'You can't do this!'

'I can. And I have.'

'Max did it for me!'

'Except this time he took the game too far.'

'I wanted you,' the actress voiced with explanatory despair. 'We have a history. We would have been good together!'

'There were no strings, Marlena.' Duardo's voice held a quality Kayla had never heard before. 'I was indebted to your father. I made him a promise. Which I kept.'

The actress burst into tears.

'No one,' he intoned with dangerous silkiness, '*no one*

attempts to harm the woman I love…and gets away with it without answering to me. Understood?'

He inclined his head, Spence opened the door and two uniformed policemen entered the room.

'What are you doing?' Marlena shrieked as they stood either side of her, caught her hands together and snapped on a pair of handcuffs.

'Arresting you, ma'am. I suggest you accompany us quietly.' They each took hold of her arms. 'It won't help if you make a scene.'

Kayla watched with a sense of stunned disbelief as the trio left, followed by Spence, who quietly closed the door behind him.

For a moment she simply stood there, then she turned slowly to face Duardo.

'What did you say?' Her voice sounded impossibly husky even to her own ears.

'You heard.'

She swallowed the sudden lump that rose in her throat. 'I think you should say it again.'

He didn't pretend to misunderstand. 'The woman I love,' he said gently, and watched as she struggled to find the words. He wanted to take her in his arms and kiss her senseless…until all the doubts and insecurities no longer existed. And he would…soon.

But first, there were things he needed to say.

'Marlena and I shared a professional relationship. Nothing more, in spite of what she liked to imply.'

He was drowning in those beautiful blue eyes, the soft, trembling mouth. *Por Dios*…all of her.

'I admired her talent as an actress. But not the games she chose to play off-stage.'

Realisation provided clarity. 'Max procured men for her.'

'Yes.'

'Except you were the unattainable prize,' she deduced slowly.

'Yes.'

He saw her moisten her lips, and the action almost undid him.

'I had you. Back in my life…my bed. No one was going to take you away from me again.'

Kayla felt the tears well behind her eyes, and she blinked them back. This was the time for truth, honesty. Not platitudes.

'I was a fool. I made the biggest mistake of my life in letting you walk away.'

'Benjamin—'

'Was a selfish, pompous ass.' She lifted a hand, then let it drop again. 'Jacob's words.'

An apt description, but one Duardo chose not to verbally endorse.

She had to ask. 'Did you deliberately seek revenge?'

'By watching you sink further into a debt you could never hope to cope with?'

'Yes.'

'Would you have accepted my help if I'd offered it?'

Stubborn pride would have forced her to refuse. Honesty made her admit it. 'No.'

'You could have asked at any time, and it would have been yours.'

Except she hadn't. Instead she'd struggled hopelessly, working harder, longer hours in order to eke out a living. Until there was no way out.

He saw the shimmer of moisture well in those vivid blue eyes, and felt his heart turn over. 'Come here.'

His gentleness undid her, and one tear escaped to roll

slowly down her cheek as she moved towards him. 'I love you. So much. I don't think I ever stopped. Even when I hated you.'

Duardo smiled at the contradiction, and caught hold of her chin between thumb and forefinger so he could tilt it towards him.

'You're the love of my life,' he vowed quietly. 'My heart, my soul. The very air that I breathe.' He brushed his lips to the tip of her nose, then slid to hover over her mouth. 'Everything. Always.'

He felt her smile as his lips settled over her own in a gentle, evocative possession that heated her body and invaded her soul.

One hand cupped her bottom as he pulled her in against the rigidity of his erection, and he threaded fingers through her hair, holding fast her nape as he went in deep.

So deep she needed to come up for air.

One look in those dark, slumberous eyes was sufficient to know mere kissing wasn't enough…for either of them.

'Any chance you can leave early?'

His smile was to die for. 'You mean you have reservations at clearing my desk and allowing me to ravish you on top of it?'

'And risk your PA witnessing her boss's complete lack of control?' She ran the tip of her tongue along his lower lip and gently nipped it. 'It would ruin your reputation.'

Duardo reached behind him and depressed a button on the inter-office communication system. 'Cancel whatever I have for the rest of the day, and transfer any important calls to my cellphone. I'll check them later.'

Much later.

He collected his laptop, his briefcase and caught her hand in his.

She waited until they were in the car and he was negotiating traffic. 'There's just one thing.'

He spared her a brief glance, caught sight of her impish smile…and waited.

'How do you feel about babies?'

The thought of her swollen with his child almost brought him undone.

Duardo changed lanes and swept to a halt at the kerb.

A soft laugh lilted from her lips. 'What are you doing?'

'This.'

He captured her face and closed his mouth over hers in a kiss that was so incredibly evocative it melted her bones.

'I take it that's a *yes*?'

The expression in those dark eyes would live with her for ever.

'Let's go home.'

If you enjoyed what you just read,
then we've got an offer you can't resist!

Take 2 bestselling
love stories FREE!

Plus get a FREE surprise gift!

THREE MORE FREE BOOKS!

HARLEQUIN *Presents*

This September, purchase 6 Harlequin Presents books and get these THREE books for FREE!

IN THE BANKER'S BED
by Cathy Williams

CITY CINDERELLA
by Catherine George

AT THE PLAYBOY'S PLEASURE
by Kim Lawrence

To receive the THREE FREE BOOKS above, please send us 6 (six) proofs
of purchase from Harlequin Presents books to the addresses below.

<u>In the U.S.:</u>
Presents Free Book Offer
P.O. Box 9057
Buffalo, NY
14269-9057

<u>In Canada:</u>
Presents Free Book Offer
P.O. Box 622
Fort Erie, ON
L2A 5X3

- -

Name (PLEASE PRINT)

Address   Apt. #

City   State/Prov.   Zip/Postal Code
098 KKL DXJP

www.eHarlequin.com